Margaret
On Her Way

The Margaret Trilogy

A Place for Margaret
Margaret in the Middle
Margaret on her Way

BERNICE THURMAN HUNTER

Margaret
On Her Way

Cover photo by Rick Buncombe

Scholastic Canada Ltd.

Scholastic Canada Ltd.
123 Newkirk Road, Richmond Hill, Ontario, Canada L4C 3G5

Scholastic Inc.
730 Broadway, New York, NY 10003, USA

Ashton Scholastic Pty Limited
PO Box 579, Gosford, NSW 2250, Australia

Ashton Scholastic Limited
Private Bag 1, Penrose, Auckland, New Zealand

Scholastic Publications Ltd.
Villiers House, Clarendon Avenue, Leamington Spa,
Warwickshire, CV32 5PR, UK

Special thanks to Don J. Mossey for his assistance with the cover photo, and to Hakim Optical for their contribution.

Canadian Cataloguing in Publication Data

Hunter, Bernice Thurman
 Margaret on her way

ISBN 0-590-73667-1

I. Title.

PS8565.U577M38 1988   jC813'.54   C88-093506-5
PZ7.H86P1 1988

9 8 7 6 5 4 3   Printed in Canada   1 2 3 4 5/9
Manufactured by Webcom Limited

For Barbara, Jean, Sonja, Vancy, Pat and Kathy

I would like to thank Dr. C.A.V. Barker, Doctor of Veterinary Science, and Professor Emeritus, University of Guelph, for his invaluable help and advice in the field of veterinary medicine.

Contents

1

Great news

The phone was ringing off the hook when I dashed in the door. I dropped my schoolbooks on the table, raced through the kitchen to the parlour and grabbed the receiver.

"Hello!"

"Is that you, Margaret?"

"Sure, it's me, Aunt Marg. Can't you tell?"

"You sound all breathless. Are you all right?"

"I'm fine. I just ran to get the phone."

I was surprised to hear from Aunt Marg, because it wasn't her usual day to phone me at the Hare's house in Shelburne. I'd been boarding there during the week for two years now while I attended continuation school, and Aunt Marg phoned me regular as clockwork every Wednesday night. Today was only Monday. In fact I'd spent the weekend at home on the farm as usual and Uncle Herb had brought me in from *Green Meadows* only the night before, so why was Aunt Marg calling me now?

"What's the matter, Aunt Marg? Is Uncle Herb sick? Is Starr hurt? Why are you phoning on a Monday?"

"Don't worry your head, Margaret. Everything's dandy here. It's just that I got a letter from your mother and I couldn't wait till Wednesday to pass on the news."

My father and my mother — Aunt Marg's sister Nellie — and my brothers and sisters (nine kids in all, not counting me) lived in Toronto on Rose Avenue, but I lived with my aunt and uncle on their farm. It was complicated having two families, but we tried our best to stay close.

"What news?"

Aunt Marg sounded tickled about something, so I was sure it wasn't bad news.

"Well, you'll never guess what I'm holding in my hand right this minute," she replied teasingly.

"No, I'll never guess, so for gosh sakes tell me."

"It's a gold-embossed wedding invitation that says Olive Eleanor Emerson is to be married July 5, 1930. Your mother wants us all to come down. I've spoken to Jessie about it already, and she says Matt's willing to take care of things here."

Jessie and Zacharia Muggins, their son Matthew and their adopted daughter Eva were our nearest neighbours and best friends.

"Oh, my gosh! Really? Olive's getting married?"

Olive was my oldest sister. She was a nurse at the Sick Kids' Hospital. I didn't even know she had a steady fella, never mind a fiancé.

"Who's she marrying, for Pete's sake?"

I felt sort of put out about being the last to know.

"Well, your mother said she took everybody by surprise, so you don't need to feel bad."

Aunt Marg could read me like a book.

"It seems she's been secretly engaged for three months now, but you know Olive. She might look the spittin' image of your mother, but she's closemouthed like your father. And maybe it's just as well, because if the hospital gets wind of it they might let her go. They're so strict about married women working, you know. Anyway, Margaret, she's marrying a young intern by the name of Andrew Webster. Your mother says he's lovely."

"What does Pa think about it?"

Olive was Pa's favourite. I knew he wouldn't give her up willingly.

"Your mother says your father is resigned. I guess that means he's happy."

"Resigned doesn't mean happy, Aunt Marg. More likely he's just accepted it."

"Well, be that as it may, Margaret. But you haven't heard the best part yet."

"The best part? You mean there's more?"

"Yes. Olive wants you and Josephine to be her bridesmaids. Now what do you say to that?"

"Really! Me and Josie? It sounds swell but . . . well . . . you know how pretty Josie is . . . and you know what I look like."

"Yes, old sweetheart, I certainly do. You're as handsome as a black-eyed Susan. You're as bright as a morning-glory. You're as — "

"Aw, you're just prejudiced," I laughed. But being compared to her favourite flowers made me feel better just the same.

"Well, love, I must ring off now. I've promised your uncle popovers tonight. Say Hello to Dora for me, and tell her I've got lots of scraps saved up for her new quilt."

Dora Hare was an incurable quilter. Aunt Marg said her work was art in it's purest form.

"I will, Aunt Marg. Give Uncle Herb my love, and tell him not to be late on Friday. I can hardly wait for the summer holidays. Take care of Starr and Silky for me." They were my horse and cat.

"I will. Never fear. Ta, ta, dear."

"Bye, Aunt Marg."

Just as I hung up, Dora came in from shopping. She was carrying a huge carton of tin goods. On the top was balanced a sack of biscuits and two loaves of bread. Dora was a town woman and didn't do her own baking and canning like Aunt Marg did.

I shoved my books aside and she hoisted the heavy box onto the table with a loud grunt.

Dora was a tall, muscular woman with a deep voice like a man. Her husband Rabbit — his real name was Roger, but everyone called him Rabbit because he could wiggle his ears and nose, and because of his last name — described her as *strapping*, so she got back at him by calling him a pipsqueak.

It took me quite a while to get used to Dora because her loud voice made me think she was mad all the time. But once I got accustomed to it, I came to really like her. As Aunt Marg always said, Dora was a good scout.

"Here, let me help you," I said, and we began putting the staples in the larder off the kitchen. While we worked, I told her about the scraps Aunt Marg had for her, to get that item out of the way, and then I told her the big news about Olive.

"Well, land's sakes, what a nice thing to look forward to, Meggie."

That's what she and Rabbit called me — Meg, or Meggie. At home I got called Peg or Peggy. Uncle Herb called me Maggie. It's amazing how many variations could be made out of just plain Margaret.

"A wedding in the family! And a pretty young

bride to boot. The last wedding Rabbit and I went to was Jasper and Beulah Streets. They tottered up the aisle as if they were on their last legs."

I laughed at the picture that flashed through my mind of the funny old couple who'd kept company for forty years and had finally tied the knot. Then right after the ceremony they'd gone back to their respective houses. Even now, they still only visited each other once a month.

"It's a peculiar arrangement, and that's a fact."

Dora knew what I was thinking.

"But if it works for them, then it's no skin off our noses."

That's the way Dora was. Nothing anybody did ever fazed her.

It'll be fun, I thought, going home to Olive's wedding. But that didn't stop me from feeling a bit leery about being a bridesmaid. I wasn't used to the limelight — except when I got in Dutch at school, that is.

Some of my teachers considered me a trouble-maker. That's because I always caught them up on their mistakes instead of keeping my mouth shut. Sometimes they complained about me to Dora.

Mr. Draggett, our physics teacher, said I was too big for my britches. Honestly, what a dumb thing to say about a fifteen-and-a-half-year-old girl!

And Miss Needle, our mathematics teacher, whose nose suited her name to a T, called me a smart aleck know-it-all.

Dora always stood up for me, though, and said I had a right to speak my mind. And as it turned out, when the report cards came out at the end of June I was vindicated. I stood first in third form — and was the youngest student by a full year too.

Anyway, I only hoped that this Andrew Webster person was good enough for my beautiful and sensitive big sister.

2
Wedding jitters

Aunt Marg made my bridesmaid dress. It was sleeveless. I begged her not to put frills around the neck and armholes, but she said it had to be the same style as Josie's. Ma had sent up the pattern and material — mauve georgette (ugh!) — so we'd both look exactly alike.

According to her, that is.

"*Nothing* could make us look exactly alike, Aunt Marg," I complained. "Josie hasn't got a freckle on her face, she doesn't wear glasses and her hair is as smooth as cornsilk."

Lately my hair, which I used to be sort of proud of because of its natural curliness, had become as coarse as a horse's tail. I couldn't do a thing with it.

"You'll both be beautiful," Aunt Marg assured me through a mouthful of pins. "Now turn yourself around."

I revolved slowly on the kitchen chair I was standing on while Aunt Marg tacked up the hem of the dress.

* * *

We arrived in Toronto right at noon hour to find poor Ma in such a state that I didn't dare complain about the dress. We'd never had a wedding in the family before and Ma was beside herself. Aunt Marg pitched right in and made us all a bite to eat.

"I don't know why you're so all-fired upset, Nell," my father complained. "I've rented the Legion Hall. They're taking care of all the jollifications."

"You did, Pa?" I'd no idea there was going to be a reception and everything.

"You betcha," he answered proudly, his thumbs hooked under his suspenders. "We've invited a hundred folks, give or take a few. We can't fit them all in here."

Not many people could afford a big wedding for their daughter in 1930 because of the depression. But my pa was luckier than most because he had a steady job at General Steel Wares. In fact, he was a boss. Ma always boasted that the factory would grind to a halt without her Will.

* * *

When the dishes were done, Josie looked at me and said, "C'mon, Peg. You and Jenny and I have an appointment at the Elegance Beauty Parlour."

"We have?" I squealed.

Boy, that raised my hopes. Maybe a professional hairdresser could do something spectacular with my unmanageable mane.

And she did. She took a long look at me and then went to work.

First she cut all the crisp, sun-dried ends off. Then, with thick, green waving lotion she marcelled my mop into deep black furrows, like a freshly ploughed field. After that she sat me under the drying machine. When I emerged, hot as a firecracker, she combed and brushed my stiff black hair into wonderful, flattering waves.

"You've got a lovely head of hair," she told me as she did magic things around my face with her fingertips.

Twirling the chair around, she held a looking glass behind me to show me how nice the back looked.

"Oh," I sighed with relief. "Thanks a lot!"

It was worth every jitney of the twenty-five cents it cost.

"You're welcome," she said with a satisfied smile. "Now you can go on your way rejoicing."

When we got home and I changed, with my new hair style even the frilly dress seemed to suit me better.

The contrast between me and Josie wasn't nearly so startling now.

In addition, I had brand new rimless glasses. Jenny said she could hardly notice them at all. Uncle Herb had insisted that I have them, even though my old ones were perfectly good. Aunt Marg said it was outlandish how he spoiled me, but she smiled when she said it.

Olive fixed her own hair in a wind-blown bob. It was shingled up the back, so all she had to do was set two big auburn kiss curls in front of each ear with bobby pins. When she combed it, out she looked just like Clara Bow in the moving pictures. And she was every bit as pretty too.

In the end, everything turned out almost perfect. Nobody tripped going down the aisle, and the best man, Rodney Gallaugher, who was handsome as the day is long, managed not to lose the ring.

Even the little kids in the family were good as

gold. All except four-year-old Patsy, that is. She was the youngest — the spitting image of Pa and me, spectacles, freckles and all.

Aunt Marg had had the foresight to tuck a bag of humbugs into her special occasions chain link purse in case Patsy should get fussy. Every time the baby opened her mouth, Aunt Marg popped a humbug into it. But instead of sucking quietly and contentedly as Aunt Marg had hoped, Patsy crunched and gulped and kept hollering for more.

Then when the clergyman said, "Who giveth this woman?" Pa looked at Olive and I knew exactly what he was thinking — what woman? This here's my little girl — and he was rendered speechless.

Two big tears trickled down the creases in his blue-shadowed cheeks and his Adam's apple bobbed up above his shiny white celluloid collar.

Ma gently put a hanky in his hand.

Dabbing under his specs and wiping his face, he finally got a hold of himself.

But instead of saying what he was supposed to, he suddenly turned on the nervous young groom and said fiercely, "Young man, do you swear you'll be good to my girl?"

Everybody in the congregation sucked in their breath and held it. You could've heard a pin drop. Only the sharp cracking of a humbug broke the silence. Poor Ma nearly died of embarrassment. Her face flushed as red as her hair.

"Will!" she hissed at Pa's back, but he just ignored her and waited for his answer.

Young Andrew Webster, who was about to become my brother if he said the right thing, looked Pa straight in the eye with the kindest expression I'd ever seen.

10

"You have my word on it, sir," he said.

As if that wasn't enough breaking with tradition, when she saw the look on Pa's face, Olive went into his arms with a little cry and laid her white-veiled head on his shoulder. Her bouquet got crushed between them, but she didn't seem to care. Then, with green eyes glistening, she stepped back into place beside her husband-to-be.

The solemn words were repeated by a bewildered clergyman, and Pa managed to say, "I do."

There wasn't a dry eye in the church. Afterwards, everyone said it was the most beautiful and touching ceremony they'd ever witnessed and they wouldn't have missed it for the world.

* * *

The reception at the Legion Hall was really something. The ladies of the Legion had prepared a splendid repast, and Ma herself had baked and decorated the three-tiered wedding cake.

Later, when all the toasting and kissing and congratulating was over, Uncle Herb and two other uncles brought out their fiddles and the music began.

Dancing was one thing I knew I was good at. Matt had taught me years ago to barn dance and square dance and polka. There wasn't a step I couldn't pick up in a minute, so I wasn't the wallflower after all. To my surprise, Josie was. She only danced once or twice and then hid behind a post and said her feet hurt. I think she was just plain scared.

As I went twirling by the ladies sitting in a row along the wall, Aunt Marg threw me a mischievous *I told you so!* look. Then, as I two-stepped merrily past the fiddlers, Uncle Herb cocked his fuzzy red head over his bow and gave me an exaggerated wink. And guess who caught the bride's bouquet? None other than yours truly!

It's funny, I thought, how things turn out exactly opposite to what you expect sometimes.

3
Gracie's turn

Gracie came home with us for her summer holidays. We took off up Rose Avenue leaving the three youngest — Davy and Bobby and Patsy — standing on the sidewalk howling their heads off as Gracie waved triumphantly out the window of our brand new Model A Ford. It was Aunt Marg who had insisted on buying the new car for the trip. She said it would be a pure disgrace to go to a wedding in a pickup.

Gracie never stopped talking the entire way. My head was spinning by the time we passed Four Corners and bumped up the long lane leading to our green farmhouse.

"Aunt Marg says I can sleep with you, Peg," she cried as she gleefully wiggled off our long-suffering aunt's lap and bounced from the running board to the ground.

"Oh, thrills!" I answered.

"Margaret! That's not nice," reprimanded Aunt Marg as she rubbed the numbness out of her knees.

She'd been holding my plump sister on her lap for sixty miles — three long hours — just so the little imp could see out the front.

"Sure, Gracie, that'll be swell," I said, trying to sound pleased.

I don't know what made me so mean sometimes. I'd been living with Uncle Herb and Aunt Marg for five years and I still didn't like to share them, especially now that I spent most of the year in Shelburne. I just wanted to keep them and Starr and Silky and everything else on the farm all to myself.

Of course, the first thing Gracie wanted to do when we arrived was learn the secret signal that only Starr and I understood. So right after supper we went out and sat on the split-rail fence together — Gracie's short fat legs pumping the air, my long spindly ones almost touching the ground.

We could see the small brown hump that was Starr's back far away on the horizon. Gracie watched fascinated as I cupped my hands around my mouth and blew with all my might. No sound came out, just a rush of air, but the big Clydesdale responded instantly.

He flung up his head, tossed his tawny mane, and came streaking like the wind across the meadow. Aunt Marg always said that it was positively uncanny how he picked up the almost silent signal.

Day after day Gracie tried to copy the soundless whistle. But like all the other kids before her, she failed. So she just had to be satisfied with a ride on Starr's broad brown back while I guided him with the flat of my hand on the side of his nose.

* * *

Two weeks is a long time to spend with your eight-year-old sister, and I have to admit, I soon found myself doing things to avoid her.

I helped Uncle Herb with the haying and mucked out the stalls in the barn and mended broken fences. I even did the milking for Aunt Marg.

Our two cows, Flora and Fancy, hated that because I didn't have Aunt Marg's special touch. They'd switch my glasses off with their tails and try to kick the bucket over when it was full. I swear they even broke wind on purpose in an effort to get rid of me.

The second week of Gracie's stay seemed endless. I thought her prattle would drive me crazy. So I spent most of my time on the roof with Uncle Herb, helping him replace the cedar shingles that had been blown off in a windstorm. I was in my glory up there in my overalls, "overhauls," as Uncle Herb called them, hammering away as we discussed everything from potato bugs to politics.

All this time, Aunt Marg was alone with Gracie. She taught her how to make baking powder biscuits and to embroider a pretty sampler and to slop the pigs — Pauline the sow had had four pink babies recently — and to "chook, chook, chook" at the chickens (better known as Aunt Marg's ladies).

It finally dawned on me that the two of them were becoming thick as thieves.

One day I came into the house unexpectedly and caught Aunt Marg giving Gracie a great big hug as she declared, "You're an old sweetheart, if there ever was one."

Instantly I saw red! *Old sweetheart* was a special nickname Aunt Marg had given me when I first came to stay on the farm. I never thought I'd live to see the day when she'd use it for anyone else.

Even though I was going on sixteen years old, I still wanted to be exclusively Aunt Marg's "old sweetheart" and Uncle Herb's "corker."

I could feel my aunt's eyes following me as I strode fuming across the kitchen and up the stairwell, slamming the door behind me. I marched into the bedroom and slammed that door too.

I propped the bedroom chair under the doorknob and flopped on my bed and stared gloomily at the ceiling.

Just then, a daddy-longlegs came prancing boldly down the wall. I waited until it was within arm's reach — and then killed it with a swat of my bare hand.

Right away I regretted my action. After all, only last week I'd had a big fight with Matt for stepping on an ant.

Now I felt even worse.

About a half-hour later, I heard a tap, tap, tapping on my door.

"Go away!" I moaned, thinking it was Gracie.

"Open up, Maggie!" ordered Uncle Herb.

Reluctantly, I got up, moved the chair, and flopped back on the bed again. He sidled in, wiggling a straw in the space between his two front teeth.

He drew the chair over and sat down next to my bed, his heavy workboots barely touching the floor. He and Aunt Marg were both short and stocky.

"Your aunt tells me you're riled about something," said Uncle Herb, pushing his specs up on top of his frizzy red head with his thumb.

He always did that when he was puzzled. He said he couldn't look and think at the same time.

"Not riled, exactly, Uncle Herb. Jealous, more like it. And I'm not very proud of myself for being jealous of a kid half my age either."

Uncle Herb stroked his stubbly chin thoughtfully.

"There ain't no age limits on feelings, Maggie," he said.

He might not know proper English, I thought, but he sure knows a lot about people.

"You must've objectified by now, Maggie, that nobody is about to take your place with your aunt and me. But that don't mean we can't take to a bright little gaffer like Gracie. She's a born mother, Mag is, and the Lord never seen fit to give us youngguns of our own, so she took to mothering her sister's brood. Seems natural enough to me."

"Aunt Marg would've made a terrific mother," I agreed.

"She's been just that to you, girl," he pointed out.

"I know, Uncle Herb, and I'm sorry if I've been a disappointment. It's just that I was born with this mean streak in me. Ma says I inherited it from my Grandma Marshall, who was as mean as an old billy goat."

"Now hold on there, Maggie. You can't go blaming your grandma. We all have to shoulder our own load."

Uncle Herb worked the straw back and forth between pursed lips, then added solemnly, "You mustn't deny your aunt the pleasure of Gracie's company. There's always room for one more in a heart as big as Mag's."

"You're right, as usual, Uncle Herb."

I sat up on the edge of the bed.

"But don't let me catch you calling her 'corker,' if you know what's good for you."

With that I gave him a playful punch in the paunch.

"Oof!" he grunted, and the straw flew out of his mouth and speared itself in my hair. Then he said, "What's that there mess on the wall?"

"Oh, that. It's a poor defenceless spider that I ruthlessly murdered instead of murdering my sister. I'll scrape it off when it dries."

"You're a corker, Maggie," he chuckled, retrieving the straw from my tangled curls. "A dad-blamed solid gold corker."

4
Dora

Gracie ended up staying at Green Meadows indefinitely.

When we took her home after a month's stay, she cried and carried on like a maniac until we promised to bring her back again. So in a way she did take my place after all.

At first I continued to resent her presence, but when I saw how happy it made Aunt Marg to have a little girl to do for again, I couldn't stay mad. And when I returned to Shelburne in September to continue my education, I was glad Aunt Marg had the company.

* * *

"Boys, oh boys, I'm glad you're back!" cried Dora as she helped me unpack my things.

"Rabbit's been complaining all summer long that the house is like a morgue without you. He hasn't wiggled his ears for a month of Sundays."

"I missed both of you, too, Dora," I said as I lined my books along the shelf that Rabbit had built over my bed.

Suddenly she leaned down and gave me a quick peck on the cheek. Dora rarely ever showed any outward sign of affection, so I was touched.

"I'll run down and finish supper while you freshen up," she said, flustered by her own display of emotion.

"I've got a nice gooseberry pie from Rachel's bakeshop just for you. It'll go good with the cream you brought."

She turned abruptly and left the room.

On my washstand stood a blue porcelain pitcher with purple flowers embossed on it. It was full of warm water and it stood in a matching bowl. A flannel towel and facecloth were neatly folded over the wooden rung on the side of the washstand. The small frame house had running water downstairs. Dora's pride and joy was her indoor water closet and bright copper bathtub. But upstairs in the attic rooms, we still used washbasins and chamber pots.

When I came down, I saw that the kitchen table — there was no dining room because the house was too small — had been laid as if for company. Dora's bone white chinaware and silver candlestick sparkled on the green linen tablecloth.

"The table looks beautiful, Dora. Just like a picture in *The Ladies' Home Journal.*"

Dora beamed at my praise.

The reason I was so thrilled with the table setting was because of the amazing contrast between that day's table and any ordinary day.

It was all I could do not to laugh out loud at the everday table. Dora had some funny eccentricities and one of her most hilarious was her habit of using newspaper tablecloths.

Every meal, she'd spread fresh newspapers over the bare wooden table. Then when we were finished supper, she'd roll them up, crumbs, spills and all, and stuff them into the stove.

"It saves a lot of fuss and bother," she explained.

I had to agree with that, but it did take me a while all the same to get used to eating off newspapers. However, once I got used to it, I found I really enjoyed it. The best day of the week was Monday. That was the day Dora used Saturday's coloured comics.

Aunt Marg nearly had a fit when she got wind of it. She said it was bad enough eating off newspapers, let alone perusing them at the table. But I didn't care. I enjoyed reading the tablecloth.

Just then, Rabbit came in from meeting the evening train. Part of his job was to pick up the mailbag and drop it off at the post office.

He grinned at me, wriggling his nose, and shot me a riddle.

"How many buckets of dirt in Blue Mountain, Meggie?"

Quick as a wink I shot back, "That depends on the size of the bucket."

"Tarnation, girl, you done it again," he hooted, slapping his knee as he made his way to the tin sink to take his teeth out and wash up for supper.

Rabbit always greeted me with a riddle instead of a Hello. And I think he'd have been really disappointed if I didn't always have an answer for him.

After a delicious supper of pork hocks and gooseberry pie, I helped Dora with the washing up. Then we joined Rabbit in the parlour to listen to the gramophone. He'd bought a packet of new needles and a brand new record just for me. It was my favourite singer, Al Jolson singing "Keep Your Sunny Side Up."

Rabbit sat right next to the Victrola in a reed

chair he'd made himself out of boiled bulrushes instead of bamboo. Every time the record slowed down and Mr. Jolson began to sound like a dying soprano singing through her nose, Rabbit would lean over and crank it up again. He played the same song over and over.

*   *   *

Dora's parlour was another of her eccentricities. Every inch of space was crowded with knick-knacks. There were china figurines, glass snowstorms, stuffed birds, pink seashells and miniature lamps with real silk shades Dora had made herself. Uncle Herb said she was a dab hand at sewing.

On a shelf that ran all around the room just below the ceiling were dozens of fancy plates standing precariously on edge. And the walls themselves were so cluttered with pictures and samplers and calendars that you could hardly see the pattern on the wallpaper.

Aunt Marg said Dora's parlour was a hodge-podge. And Rabbit called it a mess of gewgaws. But I thought it was downright interesting.

One of the samplers, signed in the corner by Dora, aged eight, particularly intrigued me. Embroidered on grey silk in neat black stitches were the words, *I wept because I had no shoes . . . until I met a man who had no feet.* The first time I read that, it made me cry.

But the sampler that hung beside it made me laugh out loud. All bordered in vines and roses, the verse read, *Women's faults are many. Men have only two. Everything they say, and everything they do.*

Dora and I sat on the cracked leather davenport that was so filled with fancy cushions you had to hold some on your lap to make room for yourself. Dora had to keep her elbows raised so her hands were free to sew the brightly coloured squares together.

We finished up the evening by having tea and pie in the kitchen.

"What's the best thing to put in a pie, Meg?" cracked Rabbit, gooseberries dripping out of the slice in his hand.

"Your teeth!" I answered triumphantly.

"Dad, blame!" he chortled, his false teeth with the orange gums clicking merrily. It was a game we played, and I was good at it.

"Well, Meggie," Dora interrupted (I guess she was sick of riddles), "how do you feel about your little sister living at Green Meadows?"

Her sudden question took me off guard. I'd always thought of Gracie as *staying* at Green Meadows, not *living* there. The more meaningful word brought me up short. A bright picture flashed through my mind of Gracie's copper-coloured hair and Uncle Herb's frizzy red curls intermingled as they shared the earphones of his crystal set the way we used to do.

My heart constricted and I was engulfed in a wave of jealousy again. Then ever so slowly, it subsided.

"I'll get used to it, Dora," I said, holding back a sigh. "I'm going to be so busy this year with four Maths, plus Latin and French, that I won't have time to think about it. Besides, I'm almost a grown woman now and Aunt Marg needs a little kid to do for. And Gracie never had so much attention in her life. They really need each other."

5
New friends

My friend Eva Muggins also boarded in Shelburne — with the Stromberg family — and I spent quite a bit of my free time there. Apart from a married daughter who lived in Parry Sound, Mr. and Mrs. Stromberg had two sons — Philbert, nicknamed the nut by his enemies and Bert by his friends, and Elliot, a fifteen-year-old cut up.

Bert was nice-looking, but not handsome. He had slick black hair with a white part down the middle that was so straight it looked as if it had been drawn with a ruler. His eyes were greeny blue, and his wide smile was only a bit spoiled by the way his two front teeth lapped over each other. But most important of all, he was taller than me!

One snowy afternoon in November, I was invited to stay for supper. Mrs. Stromberg set my place right next to Philbert. After supper, we all circled the dining room table to do our homework.

"Need any help?" offered Bert.

He was in fifth form and planning on going to university the following year.

"No thanks," I answered cockily. "I can manage."

At nine o'clock, Mrs. Stromberg insisted that

Bert walk me home, even though I said it wasn't necessary.

"Can I come too?" begged Eva, shutting her book.

"Have you finished your assignment?" asked Mrs. Stromberg.

"No, but . . . "

"Isn't it due tomorrow?"

"Yes, but . . . "

"No buts about it. Get to work. You too, Elliot."

"Rats!" said Elliot.

I got my coat on quickly.

"Goodnight. Thanks for everything," I said. Then Bert and I left.

We strolled along — self-consciously, now that we were alone — taking little slides on icy patches of the road. It was really cold for November.

Uncle Herb said the *Farmer's Almanac* predicted a long hard winter.

"Want to go to the pictures Friday night?" Bert suddenly asked as he caught his balance at the end of a frozen puddle.

Shelburne didn't have a real cinema. Instead, movies were shown at the town hall on Friday nights. They were always silent films because, as Bert explained, they didn't have the sophisticated equipment needed to show the new talkies yet. All the young people went to the "flicks" on Friday night to celebrate the end of the school week. Afterwards, everybody got together at the ice cream parlour on Main Street.

"I can't," I answered reluctantly. "I go home on Friday nights."

"Why don't you go home on Saturday morning for a change."

"Gee, I never thought of that. Maybe I could. I'll ask Dora."

"Okey-dokey," grinned Bert. "Let me know tomorrow."

The minute I stepped inside the door, I broached Dora on the subject.

"Well, Philbert's a fine fella 'n all," she said, frowning, "but you'll need to get permission from your aunt. I'll be blessed if I want to take on that responsibility."

I dropped my books with a plunk on the bare kitchen table and made straight for the parlour phone.

The Hare's telephone was the long-stemmed table type with the flared mouthpiece that looked like a black daffodil in bloom. It sat grandly on a crocheted doiley in the middle of a reed table. I picked up the horn-shaped earpiece from the hook on the side of the stem and gave Central the number. Then I heard the bells on top of the wooden phonebox in the farm kitchen jangle two shorts and two longs.

"Who might this be, calling at such an ungodly hour?" shouted Uncle Herb.

He always thought you had to yell over the telephone to breach the distance.

"Oh, Uncle Herb," I laughed, "what a way to answer! Suppose it was somebody important?"

"Sounds like somebody mighty important to me," he said. "What can I do you for, Maggie?"

"Tell Aunt Marg I have to talk to her right away. Then you come back on the line, okay?"

"Okay, corker," he answered.

I heard him shout, "You're wanted on the blower, Mag." Then I heard a muffled, "Ouch!"

I knew Aunt Marg had cracked him on his bald spot with her wide gold wedding band. She hated being called Mag, because it rhymed with hag.

"What is it, Margaret?" Aunt Marg always sounded slightly worried at an unexpected phone call, especially at night.

"Well . . ." I paused for a few seconds and then rushed ahead. "I need your permission to do something because Dora says she can't take on the responsibility."

Aunt Marg waited patiently for me to continue. Then when I didn't say anything after several seconds, she said, "For mercy sakes, Margaret, out with it!"

So I told her. She hemmed and hawed for about five minutes.

"You're only fifteen," she muttered at last.

"Nearly sixteen," I reminded her, but she paid no attention.

"I don't know if your father and mother would approve," she hedged. "And your uncle's going to be sorely disappointed if you don't come home until Saturday."

She knew that would make me think twice.

"And Gracie wants you to have a look at Silky's ear. She thinks it's infected, but I can't see a thing wrong with it."

"Gee whiz, Aunt Marg, if *you* can't find anything, how am I supposed to?"

Aunt Marg was the best nurse in the whole countryside. People trusted her even more than Doctor Tom, our country physician.

"Well, you know how Gracie looks up to you. She thinks you're a veterinarian already."

"Good grief, I'm a far cry." I was getting frustrated. "Just say yes or no and I promise I won't argue."

"Oh, I guess it'll be all right this time. But you tell that Philip Stromberg — "

"That's Philbert, but his friends call him Bert."

"Well, tell that Philbert — what an outlandish name — that you can't make a habit of it. You're needed here on the farm."

"Thanks, Aunt Marg. You're an old sweetheart."

She laughed and said, "None of your soft soap with me, my girl."

"Tell Uncle Herb to come back on the line now."

"He's standing right here beside me, 'eavestroughing,' as he would say."

The receiver changed hands and Uncle Herb bellowed, "Hello, again, Maggie. I just want to put in my two cents' worth."

"I'm ready," I sighed, expecting a bit of a lecture.

Instead he just chortled and said, "Don't do anything I wouldn't do!"

6
My first date

I was pretty excited about going out with Bert. It was my first real date with a boy. Of course, I'd been out with Matt lots of times, mostly to picnics and barn dances and hayrides, but something told me this was going to be different.

"What'll I wear, Dora?" I had my whole wardrobe spread out on the bed. Dora leaned on the doorjamb, her long face stretched in a grin.

"Wear your best bib and tucker," she advised.

"I can't wear overhauls to the town hall," I joked.

"Now you're pulling my leg," she laughed, poking a dangling hairpin into her salt-and-pepper bun. "You know I meant your Sunday-go-meeting dress."

"No. That's too fancy. Besides, I don't like frilly things. I'm too tall and gawky. I guess I'll just wear my wool jumper and middy blouse. We won't be taking our coats off anyway, because everybody says the hall is as cold as Harper's Icehouse."

Well, as it turned out, the jumper was perfect. It was so cold in the town hall you could see your breath. Not only did I not take off my coat, I didn't even unbutton it! The films were an old Laurel and Hardy comedy followed by a Felix the Cat cartoon.

I'd seen them both years before at the Bonita in Toronto, so it could've been quite boring. It wasn't, though, because Bert held my hand the entire time! Of course, we both kept our gloves on, so there wasn't much contact, but every once in a while his fingers would give mine a little squeeze. This made my heart do funny flip-flop things it had never done before.

After the movies, we went to the ice cream parlour. Mr. Blackacre made his own chocolate and vanilla ice cream in a wooden bucket outside in the snow especially for Friday nights.

Bert ordered a big chocolate soda with two straws. In order to share it, we had to put our foreheads together so that our breath steamed up my glasses. I took them off and put them in my pocket.

"Want another soda?" Bert asked. "Vanilla this time?"

I didn't really, but I did want to stay head to head with him for a while longer, so I said yes. By the time we were finished, my stomach was heaving and I quickly told Bert I thought it was time to leave.

The temperature outside must've dropped about ten degrees, but I welcomed the icy air on my face. I decided to say no to a second soda next time.

As we hurried down Rail Street, aptly named after the tracks behind it, the thin layer of snow squeaked under our feet. I slipped and almost fell, so Bert grabbed my hand — and didn't let go.

When we reached the house we lingered awkwardly for a moment outside, still holding hands. The porch light, shaped like a railroad lantern, gave off a soft amber glow.

Then as I was about to thank Bert for the swell

time, the late-night train went roaring by, blowing its crossing whistle. Rather than shout, we just smiled at each other.

What a treat it was, looking up to a boy. I was as tall, or taller, than most of the boys my age. Of course, Bert was eighteen, so I guess he was full-grown already.

Anyway, he looked nice in the dim orange light, his hazel eyes shining like a cat's, his black patent leather hair glittering with snowflakes.

Suddenly, without a speck of warning, he bent down and kissed me full on the mouth. I was so surprised, I didn't know which way to turn, so I closed my eyes — and he did it again!

All at once I felt bashful, so I lifted the latch and the front door creaked open.

Grinning, Bert jumped down the porch steps, backwards and waved goodbye from the road. Then he broke into a loping run and disappeared up the dark street.

Rabbit and Dora had gone to bed and left the hall bulb burning. I was glad they were asleep, because I knew I was blushing. Rabbit could be a terrible tease sometimes.

7

A revelation

The next day there was a terrible ice-storm, so I didn't get home until the following weekend.

On the Saturday, Gracie had her little friend Luella Raggett over to play. Then, later on in the afternoon, Mr. Muggins brought Eva over and together we worked on our geometry at the kitchen table while Gracie and Luella played old, familiar games at the far end of the room.

"Here I sit a-sewing, in my little housie," they sang in shrill, tremulous tones. "Nobody comes to see me, except my little mousie."

Eva and I exchanged nostalgic glances, sighing for our lost childhood.

"Can Luella stay all night if her mother says so, Aunt Marg?" begged Gracie.

"That might be nice, but where would Margaret sleep?"

"With me," suggested Eva. "I'll ring up Mother. I'm sure she'll say yes."

So she got Jessie's permission, and Uncle Herb let me drive to Briarwood Farm in the cutter. Starr got so excited when he saw us that it took me twice as long as usual to put his harness on.

"Sorry, old boy," I said as I put the bit in his mouth. I always apologized when I had to do that, because it seemed like such an insult to shove an iron bar between the jaws of your best friend. But the horse didn't mind. He whickered happily, tossing his mane and batting his long white eyelashes at me like the big flirt that he was.

I couldn't resist throwing my arms around his huge head and rubbing my cheek against his smooth brown jowl. Then with velvety lips he nuzzled my hair. A lump came up in my throat and I felt like a kid again.

I climbed up on the seat beside Eva and took the reins. Starr moved off at a brisk trot without being told, steam streaming back from his flaring nostrils. It had taken me so long to set off that Eva was already shivering with the cold.

"Sorry, Eva," I said, "but I haven't seen him for a whole week and we really miss each other."

"I've never known a horse to act so human," Eva said. "He actually seems to love you."

"He does. And I love him too, just as much as if he was a person. That's the main reason why I absolutely must become a vet. I've got to keep Starr alive as long as possible."

The Clydesdale pricked up his ears and switched his tail at the mention of his name, so I lowered my voice.

"He's eighteen years old, you know, Eva, and horses don't live much past twenty-five. I honestly don't know what I'd do if anything happened to him."

As we skimmed over the silvery snow and up the Muggins' lane, we saw Matt coming from the barn.

"I'll take over, Marg," he said in his warm, amiable way.

He unharnessed Starr and led him to the stable while Eva and I headed for the cosy farm kitchen.

After supper, Eva and I were helping Jessie with the washing up when Matt said, "Will you come down to the stable, Marg? I want you to take a look at Bill's right front hoof. He's been favouring it lately and I can't figure out why."

Matt too thought I was a vet already because of the way I had with animals. Aunt Marg called it an affinity.

"You two run along," Jessie said. "My daughter and I can finish up here."

Jessie was so pleased to have a daughter — she'd lost Matt's twin sister to the terrible influenza epidemic during the Great War when they were babies — that she never missed a chance to use the precious word. So I hung up the dishtowel on the wooden spokes spread out like umbrella ribs above the kitchen range and went with Matt to the barn.

By-passing Starr, who snorted his disapproval and fanned our faces with his bushy tail, we sidled into Bill's stall. Matt lifted the black gelding's hoof and I took my mitts off.

I closed my eyes and murmured soothingly as I prodded around the horseshoe with my bare fingertips. I sometimes found that my fingers were more sensitive with my eyes closed. Besides, coming in from the cold outside, my spectacles were steamed up, so I couldn't see anyway.

Suddenly I let out a yelp of pain. Bill gave a high-pitched whinny and jerked his hoof out of Matt's grip. I cleaned my glasses and peered at my finger. There was a sliver of glass no thicker than a pin poking out of a bright red bubble on my fingertip. Matt removed it gently.

Meanwhile, Bill had put his hoof down and now seemed to be standing comfortably on all fours.

"I think that's it, Marg!" Matt sighed with relief. "I'll walk him to make sure."

"It has to be disinfected first, Matt," I insisted.

Obediently, Matt fetched a bucket of well water, a brush, a cake of carbolic and a bottle of peroxide.

This time he held Bill's hoof tightly between his knees while I scrubbed and cleaned and doused it with disinfectant until the peroxide had stopped fizzing.

Then I dried the hoof with a clean flannel and finally let Matt walk my patient around the barnyard. There was no sign of a limp. Matt brought the horse back to his stall and gave him a good feed of corn and oats.

He treated Starr too of course, which helped to assuage his jealousy.

"Thanks, Marg," Matt said as we stood side by side stroking Bill's glossy black flanks.

I turned to tell him he was welcome and found that our noses were only inches apart. We were approximately the same height, so our eyes were on a level. His pale blue ones were shining into my dark brown ones.

Without a speck of a warning, he kissed me!

I was so startled I stumbled backwards, wiping my mouth with the back of my hand.

"For Pete's sake! What'd you do that for?" I snapped.

Matt's face turned beet red and he yanked his

peaked cap down over his windburned forehead to hide his embarrassment.

"Let's get out of here," I muttered, and made straight for the barn door.

There was a definite strain between Matt and me for quite a while after that, and I was truly sorry. When we were kids, Matt always used to say that we'd probably get married when we grew up, and I'd always answer, "Oh, sure!"

But now I knew we never would. Matt was more like a brother to me than a beau.

8

S.W.A.L.K.

P.O. Box 37
c/o R. Hare
Shelburne, Ont.
January 7, 1931

Dear Josie,

I haven't heard from home since Christmas, so I thought I'd write. This way you'll be forced to answer.

Everything's fine at Green Meadows. Gracie is happy as a lark and doesn't seem to miss home a bit, not even on Christmas day. What a weird kid! Of course, Aunt Marg and Uncle Herb love her to pieces and she laps it up like a kitten with its nose in a saucer of warm milk, so no wonder.

I like it here in Shelburne, but I miss Starr a lot. Dora and Rabbit are really good to me. Their only son, Angus, whom I haven't met yet, lives in Toronto now, so I guess they're lonely.

You've simply got to come up in the summertime and spend a couple of days here, Jose. You'll die laughing at Dora and Rabbit. Dora has the funniest habits. For instance, she uses newspapers instead of tablecloths on weeknights. We read yesterday's news while we eat! Sometimes we even trade pages.

Speaking of the news, isn't it awful lately? Imagine all those men out of work and having to ride the rails to Ottawa! Boy, with so many mouths to feed, I sure am glad Pa has a steady job. Aunt Marg always says we should thank our lucky stars that the depression hasn't hurt any of us personally.

Besides growing and canning everything they eat, Aunt Marg told me that Uncle Herb has a nest egg stashed away for a rainy day. His great-uncle Samuel left it to him when he went home. That's what Aunt Marg calls dying — going home!

Speaking of eggs, every Sunday when I come back from the farm I bring Dora a dozen white ones. She doesn't like brown ones even though Aunt Marg insists they're more nourishing. She always puts an extra half dozen brown ones in for me.

I also bring a gallon of milk, a quart of cream and sometimes a pie or cake if Aunt Marg has done lots of baking. I like that. Dora isn't such a good cook. For dessert she usually makes sago or tapioca pudding. I especially hate tapioca. It's like swallowing fish eyes. Ugh!

Besides all the foodstuffs, Uncle Herb also pays five dollars a week for my keep. This gives Dora some pin money.

Rabbit's nice, but he's not generous like Uncle Herb. Aunt Marg never has to ask for money. Uncle Herb says she's the boss, so she doesn't need his by-your-leave.

Rabbit is lots of fun, though, and he's always

trying to baffle me with riddles. So far he hasn't succeeded. I'll pass one of them on to you now.

"What's the best way to keep a skunk from smelling?"

Send me your answer when you write back.

Well, I've been saving my most important news till last.

Are you ready? Hold onto your hat, because here it comes.

I think I have a boyfriend! His name is Philbert Ashley Stromberg and we've been going around together quite a bit lately. Isn't that romantic? Aunt Marg thinks it's outlandish. But of course, she's a bit old fashioned. Also, she still calls boyfriends beaus. Isn't that funny?

Philbert is called Bert by his friends and, for obvious reasons, the nut by his enemies. He has straight black patent leather hair that he slicks down with brilliantine, inscrutable hazel eyes and a wide sweet smile that's only slightly spoiled by one front tooth overlapping the other.

The best thing about him is his height. He's six feet tall. Isn't that marvelous? I'm five feet seven inches in my stockings, so I tower over most of the boys I know. You're sure lucky you took after Ma instead of Pa in that department. Anyway, it's a real treat not to have to hunch over all the time.

Bert and I go to the pictures at the town hall every other Friday night, and then I go home to the farm on the Saturday morning. Uncle Herb doesn't like that much, but I can't help it. Come to think of it, Uncle Herb's been a bit cranky lately, and quiet too. I wonder what ails him?

Bert and I also go bobsledding and ice-skating. Bert made a terrific bobsled out of two small sleds — the kind children use with runners close to the ground — and a long plank and the steering wheel from an old Model A Ford. We go around the curves on Harper's hill about fifty miles an hour!

Aunt Marg doesn't know a thing about it, so don't tell Ma. They worry about the most stupid things. Bert says it's perfectly safe. Well, almost. We've flipped over once so far, but we didn't get hurt — except for a few bruises on the derriere. At least, that's where mine are!

Have you got a boyfriend yet, Josie? Will Pa let you have one? If not, don't tell him about mine, because even though I don't live at home any more, Aunt Marg says that where Gracie and I are concerned, Ma and Pa's word is law.

Write soon and tell me all the news. Does Patsy still look the spitting image of me? I hope not, poor little thing.

Your loving sister, Peg.

* * *

Just before I licked the envelope, I decided I'd better include a note to my mother and father so they wouldn't ask to see Josie's letter. Then I stuck on a two cent stamp and got Rabbit to send it for me. It would go quicker than mailing it at the post office because Rabbit would put it right on the train.

I had to wait quite a while for Josie's reply.

149 Rose Avenue
Toronto, Ontario
January 30, 1931

Dear Peg,

It was swell hearing from you. Especially about you-know-who. I told Jenny, but nobody else in the family. She's good at keeping secrets. You can't tell the boys anything.

Yes, I've got a boyfriend as well, and Ma still calls them beaus, too. Isn't that quaint? Anyway, the most coincidental thing is that my boyfriend's name is Gilbert, which rhymes with Philbert. Get it? Otherwise, there seems to be no resemblance.

Gilbert is short and cute. He's got fair hair and freckles. He reminds me a lot of Matt Muggins.

For some unfathomable reason I felt a stab of jealousy that made me feel ashamed. Perhaps it was because I knew I'd hurt Matt's feelings a lot lately on account of Bert. As far as Matt was concerned, I was like a dog in a manger. Then again, maybe it was just Grandma Marshall's nasty streak coming out in me.

Gilbert walks me home from Parkdale Collegiate every day and we go ice-skating on Riverdale Rink on Saturday afternoons. Pa won't let me go out after supper with boys yet. You're only eleven months older than me. I'll bet if you were home you wouldn't be allowed to go out at night either. So you can thank heaven you live in Shelburne.

We had a good Christmas, but we missed Gracie a lot because she's been gone only such

41

a short time, unlike you. Of course, there were just as many of us at the table, anyway, because of Andrew.

Oh, my gosh, Peg, I haven't told you the most wonderful news of all. Our Olive is in the family way. We'll soon be aunties. Can you believe it? I'm hoping for a girl, but Elmer hopes it's a boy and Jenny hopes it's one of each because she wants twins like Harry and her. Ma and Pa both say it doesn't matter a fig as long as it has all its fingers and toes.

Speaking of fingers, I hate to have to tell you this, but our Davey lost half of one of his in an accident. Mr. Gossard across the street — I don't think you know him — was cutting down a tree with a buzz saw and Davey was helping.

Well, you can picture the rest. There was blood all over the place. Poor Ma was hysterical. Too bad Aunt Marg wasn't here. She'd have known what to do. Pa was furious. He said Mr. Gossard was entirely to blame because Davey was too young to know better.

Anyway, Davey won't have a right index fingerprint any more, so it's good he's left-handed. Ma used to worry that it would be a hindrance to him all his life being left-handed, but now she says, "The Lord works in strange ways."

Patsy looks more like you every day. Pa says the two of you are cut from the same bolt — smart and sassy! Ma says the resemblance is so uncanny that she hardly misses you any more, but she doesn't mean it how it sounds, so don't take it to heart.

I'm doing okay in school. I still wish you were

here to help me, though, because I find high school hard.

Rabbit sounds like fun. With a name like that he ought to be. I give up on his riddle. What *is* the best way to keep a skunk from smelling?

Tell Dora I can hardly wait to meet her and that my favourite comics are *Freckles and his Friends* and *Tillie the Toiler.*

I'll sign off now, Peg. I have to pare the potatoes for supper. Harry's sitting right here twiddling his thumbs but Ma says he doesn't have to help with supper because he's a boy. What a dumb reason!

Give my love to everybody, especially Uncle Herb. I can't imagine him being cranky. Maybe he's just getting old.

Everybody sends their love, especially Ma and Pa. Pa just came in the door from shovelling the sidewalk.

Uh, oh, he just said he's about had enough of shovelling snow, so I asked him why he didn't make Harry do it. If looks could kill I'd be dead!

Jenny says she'll write soon and Patsy kissed the corner of this page.

As ever, Josie

Sure enough there was a lip-shaped jam splotch on the right-hand corner that made me forgive Patsy instantly for taking my place at home.

9

Double trouble

"Why don't the corn like the farmer?" asked Rabbit with a twitch of his knobby nose.

"Because he picks their ears!" I shot back.

"Dag-nab it, girl."

He scraped the chair back from the table, his ears going a mile a minute.

"One of these days . . . "

"I'll have to remember to ask Josie that one," I said with a smile.

"Well, if you want my opinion, I think it's disgusting," snapped Dora as she rolled up the newspapers and stuffed them into the fire. "It's just a mercy we're done eating."

Laughing, I got the graniteware dishpan down from the nail on the wall and set it in the tin sink. I filled the pan with dipperfuls of warm water from the stove's reservoir, then swished the wire soapcage around to make some suds.

"Just leave the dishes to soak," Dora said with a sharp edge to her voice. "I want a word with you."

The minute Rabbit caught her change of tone, he beat it out the back door, muttering something about unfinished business at the railway station.

I sat down opposite Dora, my mind flitting

around like a butterfly, trying to settle on what I'd done wrong.

Dora wasn't one to mince words.

"Your exams begin soon. Isn't that right?"

"Yes."

I was immediately on the defensive.

"Well, miss, it's one thing to outwit Rabbit and his foolish riddles, but that means nothing when it comes to school work. They don't give marks for that on your report card. Don't you think it's high time you started knuckling down?"

"What for?" I answered boldly. "I'm not behind in anything."

"That's as may be. But sometimes it's them that thinks they're so clever that gets their comeuppance."

Dora kept her eyes down, drumming her fingers agitatedly on the table.

"Your aunt and uncle would be dastardly disappointed if you let spooning interfere with your school work."

Spooning? Good grief!

"Oh, Dora, don't worry," I said, relieved and offended simultaneously. "I'll go over my notes on the weekend."

"You'd better do more than just go over your notes," she huffed as she got up and started washing the dishes.

*   *   *

The following Friday night I was due to go to the picture show with Bert, and I wasn't about to let school work get in the way of my biweekly entertainment at the movies. This time they were playing a Rudolph Valentino film that was so old-

45

fashioned that everybody roared with laughter at the sad parts and hissed and whistled through the love scenes.

Then right in the middle of the show the screen went black and the lights came on. Everybody began to stomp their feet and yell in protest and a boy named Horace Barwinkle pulled a beanshooter out of his windbreaker pocket and started blowing bee-bees in all directions.

Suddenly one of the little metal pellets creased my forehead. Then, before I had time to even yell, another one hit my right lens dead centre. The sharp *CRACK* so close to my ear sounded like a window breaking.

Outraged, I took my broken spectacles off to examine them — and found blood all over the frames. More blood began to trickle down my face, and with a little cry I clutched frantically at my forehead.

Instantly, Bert lunged at Horace and the two of them landed in a thrashing heap on the floor. Mr. Stromberg, who'd volunteered to be our chaperone and to run the projector, grabbed the two of them by the hair and yanked them apart.

As it turned out, I'd shut my eyes in the nick of time, so I'd actually received nothing worse than a bruise to my forehead and a minor cut over my right eye. Still, Dora was mad as a hatter when she saw me.

"Serves you very well right," she grumbled as she tore a strip off an old bedsheet and wrapped it none too gently around my throbbing head. "You never pay me no mind."

She was so crotchety that night that I was

thankful when Mr. Muggins came to pick me up the next day.

Aunt Marg nearly had a fit.

"Oh, Margaret!" she cried as she carefully unwound the makeshift bandage.

"Another half-inch and you might've been blinded."

After cleaning the cut with a carbolic acid solution, she daubed it with iodine. It stung like anything, but I didn't let on.

"I don't think you should go to that town hall any more. You don't belong with those hooligans."

"They're not hooligans, Aunt Marg," I assured her as she applied a neat patch. "It was just an accident."

Uncle Herb peered over the top of his specs and tried his best to look severe.

"You'd better high-tail it into Arnold Sparke's shop first thing Monday morning, Maggie," he said. "Tell him I'll settle with him on Friday when I come to fetch you."

Arnold Sparkes was the town optometrist.

"Oh, golly," I said, turning my head away. "That'll be my third lens this year. I'm sorry to cause so much expense, Uncle Herb."

"Speak up, Maggie. I can't hear you when you mumble like that," Uncle Herb said, cupping his right ear towards me.

I thought I'd spoken perfectly clearly, but nevertheless, I repeated what I'd said in a louder, clearer voice.

When Uncle Herb realized what I'd said, he brushed my lament aside with a smile and a wave of his hand and I thought the whole affair was forgotten and done with.

I didn't miss my glasses too much until I went to school on the Monday. Then I discovered that I had to settle for just listening to the lessons. It was useless to even try to read what was on the blackboard. And at the supper table that night the Saturday comics were just a colourful blur under my plate.

To make matters worse, it took a whole week to get my special prescription made. Mr. Sparkes said he had to go all the way to Toronto for them. And it was lucky for me he had other business there, or it would have cost Uncle Herb and arm and a leg.

10

Comeuppance

The following Sunday night, Bert phoned and asked me to go bobsledding.

"*NO!*" barked Dora before I even had a chance to speak. She must be clairvoyant, I thought miserably as I turned my back on her and made a face into the phone. Bert had heard her answer too, so after a whispered conversation we hung up.

As soon as I put the phone down, Dora asked in icy tones, "Don't your examinations start on Wednesday?"

"Yes."

"Then get at your books!" she snapped.

Sulkily I unstrapped my books and set to work. About an hour later, Dora silently set a cup of strong tea and a buttered scone beside my algebra book. I thanked her and she took herself off to bed.

I hate to admit it, but Dora was right. They don't give marks for solving riddles. All that week I crammed belatedly for my exams, but it was too little too late. To my shame, I received the lowest average of my life — seventy-two percent.

Not only that, but I was tenth in the class, a placing that I considered a pure disgrace.

"That's not so bad," commiserated Eva, "when

you think how long you had to go without your glasses."

"Shoot!" exclaimed lackadaisical Elliot Stromberg. "If I got a mark like that, I'd think I'd died and gone to heaven."

But their words were cold comfort to me.

* * *

It was the first time in my life that I was ashamed to hand my report card to Aunt Marg and Uncle Herb.

They studied it together in silence.

Finally Uncle Herb said quietly, "You'll need to do better than that if you plan on being a vet, Maggie."

The disappointment in his voice nearly killed me.

"No more Philip Stromberg for you, my girl," ordered Aunt Marg.

Gracie looked from one to the other, dumbfounded. Wordlessly, she placed Silky on my lap.

The cat crawled up my sweater to my shoulder and began licking my face with her pink, sandpaper tongue. Then she curled herself around my neck like a soft fur collar and started to purr. I scratched between her ears. Even though she belonged to Gracie now, I still think she remembered the time I risked my neck and broke my leg to save her when she was stranded high up in a tree.

"Don't worry," I assured them, "it won't happen again."

And it didn't. I worked like a Trojan for the rest of the school year and never so much as glanced at a boy. In fact I was so busy that I hardly even noticed when winter turned into spring. One minute the meadow was covered in snow, then the next thing I knew it was sprinkled with purple violets.

The final exams lasted a solid week. When they were over, I knew I had outdone myself. But the results surprised even me. I had actually earned my junior matriculation with a ninety-five per cent average.

Dora was flabbergasted.

"I thought my Angus was clever," she said, staring at me as if I'd been transformed like a chameleon overnight, "but beside you, girl, he don't hold a candle."

"Oh heck, Dora, anybody can do it if they work hard," I said.

I tried not to sound too proud of myself, because I knew it wasn't all my doing.

When I had told Bert that I couldn't date (the newest word for courting) until the end of June, he had dropped me like a hot potato. Then I started to hear rumours through the grapevine that he had been seen lollylagging all over town with a blonde girl by the name of Belinda Barwinkle, Horace Barwinkle's sister.

Belinda was a cute little thing with big dimples and round blue eyes. She was only five feet tall, so she stared up at Bert adoringly. And he loved it, the silly article.

So, to keep my mind from thinking about them, I studied like mad, so in a way, Bert helped me get my high marks.

And I got my comeuppance, as Dora would say, twice.

11
Summer, 1931

Gracie and I only spent one week of the summer holidays at home in Toronto. Uncle Herb and Aunt Marg were too busy to leave the farm, so we went by train.

Ma was tickled pink to have us. And the nicest thing happened while we were there. Olive had her baby! It was a boy weighing eight pounds.

Olive was lying in at the Women's College Hospital. They had very strict regulations. No one was allowed to visit the new mother except *her* mother, and her husband. Pa was fit to be tied when he heard that.

"After all," he growled, "Andrew isn't even a blood relation."

Anyway, by telling her I'd come from out of town, Ma sweet-talked the head nurse into letting me see Olive. She managed to make it sound like I'd just flown in from Timbuktu.

I was amazed to see that motherhood hadn't changed my oldest sister the least little bit. In fact she seemed more beautiful than ever.

"Did you see the baby?" she asked, her face all aglow.

We'd stopped at the nursery on the way in.

"Isn't he gorgeous? He's just like Andrew, except for my red hair."

"He's pretty as a picture," Ma agreed, thrilled to pieces with her first grandchild.

"He sure is. He's going to be a real lady-killer when he grows up," I said. "Have you named him yet?"

"Yes. William Emerson, after Pa," Olive announced solemnly. "And I want him called William, not Will."

She looked pointedly at Ma when she said this, because Ma always called Pa "Will" for short.

"William Emerson Webster. That's a swell name. Pa must be proud as Punch."

Just then a woman wearing a white smock over a blue checkered housedress came breezing into the room. She looked like any ordinary woman except for the stethoscope around her neck.

Olive introduced us.

"This is Dr. McIntyre, Peggy. My husband is studying under her. This is my sister, Peg — I mean, Margaret — Emerson."

The doctor's eyes lit up.

"Aren't you the girl who's broken leg I set in Sick Children's Hospital? The girl who wants to be a veterinarian?"

I was thrilled that she remembered me.

Popping a thermometer under Olive's tongue, she pressed Olive's wrist with her fingertips.

"My father, God rest his soul, was a veterinarian. When I showed an inclination towards medicine, he backed me all the way — against a great deal of opposition, I might add."

She removed the thermometer and read it with satisfaction, then snapped it down repeatedly.

"I know what you mean," I sighed. "Nobody takes girls seriously when they say they want to be a doctor. My teachers are always trying to discourage me."

"Well, don't let them!"

Her eyes sparked with indignation. Then she added briskly, "I must be on my way. I've got twenty babies to attend to, including one beautiful redheaded boy."

Ma and Olive fell for that line like a ton of bricks.

Before she left, the doctor turned and looked me straight in the eye.

"Margaret," she said. "A word to the wise. You must ignore the doomsayers and forge full steam ahead. Remember, it's your life. Good luck!"

And with that, she whisked out the door and down the corridor, her white coat billowing out behind her.

"There now, Peggy," declared Ma proudly. "You see. You can be anything you want to be. And a plague on those who say you can't."

Knowing a fullfledged woman doctor was certainly an inspiration to me. But seeing Olive's radiant face made me want to be a mother too. I didn't know how I was going to do it, but I was determined to be both.

*   *   *

The day before Gracie and I went back to Four Corners, Olive came home with William. She was going to stay with Ma for a week or so until she got on her feet.

The whole family was ecstatic. The little kids hung over the cradle, sticking their fingers in the baby's tiny fist and touching his downy red hair. Even Elmer, who was shy of babies, held him once or twice.

I thought Ma and Pa would've had their fill of kids, what with ten of us, but they seemed overjoyed to have a grandson. Mind, I noticed Pa still made his escape down to his den in the cellar right after supper, just like always.

Anyway, I was glad Gracie had seen William before we left, or she'd have been mad all the way home.

Davey came back with us for his holiday because it was his turn. And Bobby and Patsy yelled their heads off at being left behind again.

When we got back, it was the funniest thing to see Gracie showing off to Davey as if she was a veteran farmer. She even pretended not to be afraid of Starr.

And there was another thing I noticed about her. She didn't get upset every time Aunt Marg hugged Davey or called him pet names like bright eyes or sunny boy. Gracie didn't seem to have a jealous bone in her body.

She was so good-natured that Uncle Herb nicknamed her his sweet petootie. The difference between sweet petootie and corker was pretty obvious. I guess that unlike me, Gracie hadn't inherited Grandma Marshall's nasty streak.

12
Another new babe

Right at the beginning of the summer, Uncle Herb's hired man quit all of a sudden and went out west to seek his fortune. Uncle Herb said that was about as dumb as going to the north pole for a suntan!

Anyway, since he was short-handed, I pitched in with everything. I even helped Dr. Wiley with the calving.

Aunt Marg thought it might be too much for me — seeing Fancy in distress, that is — but I managed to soothe the young cow's fears and keep her calm while Doc Wiley did the work.

Oh, what a thrill it was to see that helpless little creature come slithering into the world. I watched fascinated as her skinny wet legs unfolded. She reminded me of a fern uncurling in springtime, so I instantly christened her Fern.

All our cows had names beginning with the letter F. There was poor Fauna, who'd choked to death on a turnip back in 1926, and Flora (Uncle Herb referred to her as the old girl now, but she still gave plenty of milk), and Fancy, Flora's daughter. And now, pretty doeeyed Fern, Flora's granddaughter.

While Doc took care of Fancy, I gently wiped the calf down and then gave her to her mother.

About a half-hour after the birth, both mother and daughter were on their feet. The little brown heifer stood on trembling legs, leaning on her mother. Then she began to bunt under Fancy with her pink wet nose in search of sustenance.

"She's pretty wobbly yet," laughed Dr. Wiley as he washed up in the bucket of soapy water Aunt Marg had brought out for him, "but she's a fine calf and it won't be long before she's as strong as her mother."

"How did I do, Doc?" I asked anxiously as he packed his instruments carefully into his worn leather satchel.

"You're a regular trooper, Maggie," he answered. "I just hate to think what'll become of my practice when you hang out your shingle."

I blushed with pride.

"Aw! I'll never be as good a vet as you."

But I knew I would. My heart was set on it. And Uncle Herb always maintained that when I made up my mind about something, I was as stubborn as McGogerty's mule.

I was flattered at the compliment, but not terribly thrilled with the form it took!

That night after supper I started to help with the washing up, when Aunt Marg took the dishrag out of my hand.

"You sit yourself down, girl. You've done enough for one day. Here, Gracie, you dry. And, Davey . . .

"For mercy sakes, child, what're you doing?"

Davey was standing on his head against the wall, his straight brown hair spread out like a fringed mat on the floor.

"I'm seeing if my supper will come back up," he replied cheerfully.

"Well if it does, guess who's job it'll be to mop the floor?"

At that, Davey did a quick back flip and was on his feet in a second.

"You put the dishes in the cabinet, Davey. There's a good boy. Your sister looks all done in."

"Thanks, Aunt Marg. I sure am tired."

I collapsed into the rocking chair, my legs as wobbly as the newborn calf's.

"I think I'll listen to the crystal set for a while. It'll help me relax."

I reached behind me for the earphones that hung on the knob of the chair.

"That set ain't worth a hoot any more, Maggie," remarked Uncle Herb, twirling a straw in rapid circles between his teeth.

I adjusted the headset over my ears and listened. To my surprise I picked up W.I.P. in Philadelphia just as plain as if it was coming from Shelburne.

"It sounds swell to me, Uncle Herb. There's a man talking to Colonel Charles Lindbergh about his solo airplane ride across the Atlantic. Come and listen."

He sat down and I put the earphones over his fuzzy red head and kissed his bald spot. I used to do that a lot when I was a little kid.

He puckered his brow, concentrating. Then he began to jiggle first one earphone and then the other. After about five minutes, he yanked them off impatiently and handed the headset back to me.

"It's faded out again, Maggie. Mebbe it'll come back in tomorrow night."

I put the headset on again and found to my surprise that the station was still perfectly clear. Now a high tenor voice was singing a slow melody.

* * *

Right about then, I must've fallen asleep sitting up, because the next thing I knew it was morning and I was in bed beside Gracie.

"How did I get here?" I wondered aloud.

Gracie laughed her high-pitched giggle.

"We sleepwalked you up to bed and Aunt Marg put your nightshift on over your underwears."

"Swell!"

I flung back the summer quilt and bounded out of bed.

"That'll make it all the easier to get dressed. C'mon, Gracie, let's get Davey and go check on Fern."

We went down to the barn and spent the whole morning coddling Fancy and her baby.

On our way back to the house, Davey said, "Peggy, Gracie says that when you were our age, you used to play tricks on Uncle Herb. Will you show us how to play a trick?"

"Hm," I pondered, "I'll have to think about that, Davey. Uncle Herb knows all my old tricks, so we'd have to think up a brand new one."

"Did you ever play a trick on Aunt Marg?" asked Gracie.

"Once."

I grinned at the memory that popped back into my mind.

"Ma had sent me two celluloid eggs full of jellybeans for Easter. When I'd eaten all the candies, I wondered what to do with the eggs. They snapped together in the middle and looked like real eggs. Then I got an idea. I sneaked out to the henhouse and tucked them under two of Aunt Marg's ladies. Well, when she gathered the eggs that day she must've been preoccupied about something, because she didn't even notice the difference in weight. It wasn't until the next morning at breakfast when she tried to crack them open on the edge of the frying pan that she realized she'd been fooled."

"What'd she do?" squealed Gracie.

"Was she mad?" grinned Davey.

"No, she wasn't mad. She laughed her head off. But she didn't let me get away with it. She made me gather the eggs every day for a whole week."

Gracie and Davey were still laughing when we walked in through the woodshed door.

"Wash your hands at the basin," said our practical aunt, ignoring the giggles.

But Uncle Herb said, "What's the big joke?"

"That's for us to know, and you to find out," I said, giving Gracie and Davey a conspiratorial glance.

They snickered and snorted all through dinner, but they didn't tell.

13
A brand new trick

That night after supper, Uncle Herb went out to sit on the piazza. Tipping back a weather-beaten old kitchen chair, he balanced it on its wobbly legs, propped his feet up on the railing and began to chew to his heart's content. It was downright fascinating to see him spit through the space between his two front teeth and hit a yellow daisy right in the eye at ten paces.

The next day while he was still out in the field haying, Aunt Marg came back from the barnyard after feeding her ladies. I was in the kitchen laying the table for supper when I heard her let out a screech that made me jump a mile.

"What's the matter, Aunt Marg? Did you get stung by a bee?"

"My daisies! My glads! My delphiniums!"

Aunt Marg had dropped to her knees and was cupping wilted flowers in her hands.

"For mercy sakes, what ails them?" she mourned as the petals came off in her fingers.

"Why, they're all over brown spots. They look like they've got the blight."

She held a sickly flower to her nose and sniffed. Suddenly she knew.

"That man!" She rose up to her full five feet,

giving her apron an angry shake. "That husband of mine. Just wait until I get my hands on him."

When supper was ready, Gracie and Davey fought over who'd ring the dinner gong. Then Uncle Herb came whistling in the door as innocent as a spring lamb.

"HERBERT ALFRED WILKINSON!"

The second Uncle Herb heard Aunt Marg use his full name like that, especially in such a stentorian voice, he knew he was in for it.

"What in thunder did I do now?" he growled defensively.

"You've killed my whole flower bed, that's what you've done. You and your vile tobacco habit."

I was on her side this time, because I hated to see anything killed, even flowers.

We ate our stew in stony silence. Even Gracie kept quiet. Davey studied his finger stub the way he always did whenever he was perturbed about something, almost as though he thought it might be about to sprout.

Uncle Herb hurried through his supper and went skulking off to the barn.

"Aw, poor Uncle Herb," I said to Aunt Marg, my heart melting. "I'm sure he didn't mean any harm."

"I know you think he's a paragon, Margaret. And bless my soul, so do I most of the time. But he's got to be taught a lesson."

I'd been thinking about the problem all through supper, and I'd finally come up with an idea.

"Do you still want to play a trick on Uncle Herb, Davey?"

"Ya! Ya!" cried my mischievous little brother.

Aunt Marg was filling the dishpan with dipperfuls of warm water.

"What've you got up your sleeve this time, Margaret?"

She sounded like her old self again.

That was the nicest thing about Aunt Marg. She never stayed mad for long.

"Let's make an imitation tobacco plug that looks so real Uncle Herb won't know the difference until he starts to chew. One that'll taste so bad he'll never get over it."

"What'll we make it out of?" squealed Gracie, hopping from one foot to the other.

"I know!" Davey dove headfirst into the woodbox and came up with a piece of wood about the right size.

"Davey! D'you want to break Uncle Herb's teeth?"

"Well, what'll we use, then?"

He plunked the wood back into the box, scaring Silky, snoozing under the stove. She yowled and spat at him.

"How about a chunk of carbolic soap smeared with brown shoe polish and wrapped in *Old Plug* paper?" I suggested as I dried the spoons and dropped them clinking into the spoon jar in the centre of the table.

"That's no good. He'll smell it!" cried Gracie, almost dropping a dish in her excitement.

"That's right. He will," agreed Aunt Marg. "Shoe cream would be a dead giveaway."

The problem nearly had me stumped. Then I got a flash of inspiration.

"I think I've got it," I said, pausing dramatically.

Gracie and Davey waited impatiently for me to go on, nearly beside themselves with expectation.

"We'll rub real tobacco into the soap until it's completely camouflaged."

Instantly there was a chorus of agreement. Quickly we cleared the table. Aunt Marg fetched the cake of carbolic while I went to the woodshed and snitched a plug of tobacco from the pile.

I cut the soap and showed Davey how to roughen the smooth surface with a fork while I carefully unwrapped the tobacco plug so as not to rip the paper. Then Gracie and I took turns rubbing it into the soap. When we were finished, it looked and smelled exactly like the real thing.

Following the original creases, I wrapped our fake tobacco plug neatly in the paper and hid what was left of the genuine plug in the woodbox. I just had time to set the fake plug on top of the pile when Uncle Herb came sidling into the house through the woodshed door.

He took himself straight off to bed.

The next night at the supper table, we all acted perfectly natural. Gracie and Davey jabbered a mile a minute, Uncle Herb and I discussed the crops and Aunt Marg declared proudly that her ladies had produced a record number of brown eggs.

Then Aunt Marg and I started the washing up. That was Uncle Herb's cue to sneak out to the woodshed, grab a plug from the top of the pile and head for the piazza.

This time he placed his chair on the opposite side of the porch, facing the trellis of morning-glories.

"Well, for land's sakes," sputtered Aunt Marg indignantly as we all peeked through the curtains. "Now that scoundrel's going after my glories."

We watched breathlessly as he began his ritual.

First he peeled the paper off, then he drew the plug under his nose to savour the aroma.

"If it passes the sniff test," chuckled Aunt Marg, "we're home free!"

Our soapy plug must've passed, because he snapped open his penknife and proceeded to carve off a corner.

"Oh, my gosh," I hissed. "He'll notice it's white inside."

Gracie and Davey sucked in their breath. The suspense was killing us all, but we needn't have worried. Uncle Herb was too busy daydreaming to pay any attention.

From the dull side of the knife, he popped the soap into his mouth and began to chew.

Suddenly he leapt to his feet, toppling the chair, and began frantically hacking and spitting over the railing.

"Argh!"

He gagged and coughed and choked and spat, wiping his mouth furiously on his shirt sleeve. The four of us dissolved into stitches. Then the screen door banged open and a red-faced, outraged Uncle Herb exploded in.

"WHY YOU . . . YOU . . . YOU . . . DOD-GASTED, COLD-BLOODED, ORNERY CRIT-TERS! YOU'RE OUT TO POISON A MAN!"

Gracie and Davey danced around him like whirling dervishes.

"We did it, Uncle Herb! We did it! Are you mad?"

Aunt Marg and I didn't hear his answer because we were laughing so hard we both had to race down the path to the outhouse. When we came back, Uncle Herb was gargling and gurgling at the basin.

Suddenly I felt remorseful, so I gave him a squeeze from behind.

"It's for your own good, you know," I said affectionately. "Dr. Tom says chewing tobacco is bad for the digestion."

"Well carbolic's a dang sight worse."

Uncle Herb's voice was muffled by the flannel as he scrubbed his tongue.

"I'm sorry, Uncle Herb."

Gracie's face was all puckered up, as if she was going to cry.

"Me too!" agreed Davey, giving Uncle Herb's leg a bearhug.

"Well, you're a passle of no account corkers, the lot of you. Especially that one."

He glared ferociously at me.

"Don't look at me!" I protested innocently. "It wasn't my idea to play a trick on you."

"You can't bamboozle me, Maggie Rosie Emerson. A prank like that's got your stamp all over it."

Still wiping bubbles from his bewhiskered chin, he went on muttering to himself, "Dad-blamed no-karat corkers."

It was the last childish trick I ever played on my sweet uncle, and the meanest. It would've been worth it, too, if it'd worked, but all it did was put a cramp in his style.

Anyway, Davey had some swell stories to take home to tell the family.

14

A chat with Starr

"Well, Starr, I'm off to school again," I said as I rode the big Clydesdale into the bush lot on the far side of the pasture.

Matt and I had gotten lost in the bush lot once when we were kids, and Starr had saved our lives. It'd been dead of winter and we would've frozen to death for sure if my beloved horse hadn't responded to the secret signal. Now I knew every link and chain that made up Green Meadows farm like the back of my hand and I couldn't lose my way if I wanted to.

"I'm really anxious to get started on my senior year, because after that comes the Ontario Veterinary College in Guelph. Then I'll be on my way to becoming a real animal doctor. In the meantime, don't you dare get sick."

I scrunched down and ducked my head as we passed under some low-hanging branches.

"Are you listening to me, boy?"

Starr craned his neck around, twitched his long pointed ears and swept his snowy lashes over his shining dark eyes. Then he puffed out his velvety lips and blew a low vibrating whicker.

Oh, how I love that shimmying, horsy sound!

Stretching myself full length along the crest of

his strong neck, I clasped my hands under his smooth brown jowls and buried my face in his golden mane. After working and playing with him all summer long I was sure going to miss him.

* * *

Uncle Herb drove me into Shelburne on Labour Day. The pickup trundled down bumpy Rail Street and soon we could see Dora outside stooped over her bit of a flower bed.

The truck came to a stop with a squeal of brakes amidst billowing dust. Dora straightened up, rubbing her long spine as she did so, a bunch of purple zinnias in her hand.

"Well, speak of the devil!"

She laid the flowers on the porch steps and wiped her muddy hands on her pinafore.

"I just now said to my Angus, 'I hope Meggie gets here before you leave.' "

"Angus is here?"

I'd been dying to meet her only son.

"Yep. Been home nigh on two weeks. He's away again right after supper. I've got pot roast, string beans and bread pudding. Would you care to stop and have a bite with us, Herb?"

"Don't mind if I do!" declared Uncle Herb, licking his chops as if he hadn't just polished off a full course dinner at noon hour.

"I'll just give Mag a ring on the blower."

He hopped down from the cab and got my grip from the back. Then he hoisted two big boxes of books over the side and set them on the grass with a grunt.

Just then, the screen door clacked open and out

onto the porch stepped the living image of Gilbert Roland, the moving picture star.

"This here is my son, Angus," Dora said proudly.

"Angus, this is my star boarder Margaret Rose Emerson. Course, you two men know each other."

Uncle Herb shook his head in amazement.

"I never would've knowed you, boy. You've changed and growed so much, I'd have passed you on the street."

Angus ignored Uncle Herb's observation.

"How are you, sir," he said, clicking his heels and bowing from the waist.

I'd never seen anyone do that before, so I was impressed.

"Now, don't you go calling me sir, young fella. You know my name and I ain't been knighted by the king since last we met."

Dora's son didn't even so much as *hint* at a smile in response to my uncle's cheery admonition.

Darn, I thought, gazing at Angus's incredibly handsome profile. If only I'd worn a decent dress! And my hair. I should've been fixing it instead of combing Starr's tail. And my freckles! Aunt Marg warned me about not wearing my straw hat in the hayfield.

"How do you do, Miss."

Angus offered me a limp, lily-white hand and my heart did somersaults. Beside him, Bert Stromberg looked like a bucktoothed beaver.

"Pleased to meet you, Angus," I said in a breathy voice. "Your mother's told me all about you."

Our fingers had barely touched before he drew

his away. I guess my hand felt rough compared to his.

He didn't say any more, so Dora and I picked up the boxes and Uncle Herb carried my grip into the house.

Angus didn't offer to help.

Rabbit was sitting on a stool beside the Kitchen Queen range, contentedly carving himself a chunk of *Old Plug*. He cut off the kitty-corner and tendered it to Uncle Herb on the dull side of the knife. Dora allowed chewing in the house. They even had a spittoon in the parlour next to the Quebec Heater, though I'd never seen Rabbit actually use it.

"What's the best way to ketch a fish, Meggie?" That's how Rabbit greeted me after not seeing me for two months.

"Have somebody throw it to you!" came my reply.

"Dad-blame it, girl!" he snorted with delight. "I'll fool you one of these days."

Wiggling his ears and nose simultaneously, he lifted the stove lid and sent a stream of brown juice sizzling into the fire. Angus grimaced and turned away. I laughed and picked up my grip and headed upstairs to my bedroom.

In the corner of the room by the door, all strapped and buckled, sat a big leather suitcase. It hadn't occurred to me that Angus would stay in the room I stayed in. It gave me a funny turn — a sort of dispossessed feeling.

I lay down on top of the starburst quilt for a minute to reclaim my territory. The felt mattress seemed to sag in the middle, so I hung my head over the side and looked underneath. Sure enough, one of the wooden slats was broken.

With a sigh I got up and tidied my hair, cleaned my specs and changed my dress. Then I put some lip rouge on.

Eva had given me a stick for my last birthday, but I hadn't used it yet. Most of the girls in high school used lip rouge — in addition to cheek rouge and face powder. They were always sneaking their puffs out behind their books to powder their noses. But I hadn't bothered yet.

"MEGGIE!"

Dora's strident voice came sailing up the stairwell.

"Supper is served!"

Supper is served?

I'd never heard Dora say that before. Her usual cry was, "Soup's on!"

The table was set with the green linen cloth, silver cutlery and white china dishes. In the centre, in a cut glass vase, the purple zinnias that Dora had been picking when we arrived added a nice touch of colour.

"How's the new job, then?" asked Uncle Herb as he helped himself to a huge dollop of mashed potatoes.

"Splendid, thank you, sir," answered Angus grandly. "The Transportation Commission chose me over hundreds of other applicants."

"It's no picnic landing a good job in these hard times," interjected Dora proudly as she served her son the choicest cut of meat.

"And they give him a uniform, and put him on the day shift straightaway."

I wondered what was so special about the day shift. My Pa worked nights half the time, and he was a boss.

"I'm drawing fourteen dollars a week," bragged Angus as he cut his meat into dainty, bite-sized pieces. "*Plus* overtime. And a week's summer sabbatical, *with* recompense."

Sabbatical! Recompense! He sounded as if he'd swallowed a dictionary.

Suddenly he turned his attention to me and what looked like a smirk seemed to flit across his face.

"What about you, young lady? With that crop of freckles, your ambition must surely be to marry a farmer."

He couldn't have said anything worse if he'd thought for a week. And I was sure I detected a sneer in the way he said farmer.

My face blazed and a sarcastic reply jumped to my lips. I had to bite my tongue to keep it in.

When I'd gotten hold of my temper, I answered coldly, "If I do get married, I *will* choose a farmer."

Across the table, Uncle Herb was straining forward, cupping his ear, so I raised my voice a notch.

"But my ambition is to become a veterinarian, and I don't think I'll have time to do both."

"Maggie's just past sixteen," bragged Uncle Herb, "and already she's going for her senior matriculation."

"She'll be the youngest scholar in fifth form," added Dora, anxious to make up for her son's rudeness.

"She's quick as a whip, that one. You won't find no flies on her."

Rabbit waggled his fork in my direction to emphasize his words and accidentally flicked gravy on Angus's immaculate coatsleeve.

"Oh, no!" yelled Angus.

Leaping to his feet, he stuck out his arm as if a bird had dropped something on it.

"You careless fool!" he snarled at his father. "Now see what you've done."

Dora jumped up like a shot, rushed over to the sink and came back with a wetted flannel. Nervously she began sponging the greasy brown splotch.

Angus brushed her away impatiently.

Rabbit just ignored the whole scene and picked up a juicy bone with his fingers. After a few chews, he put the bone down, poured tea from his cup to his saucer, blew waves across it and drank it down in one loud slurp. I'd never known him to use such bad manners before.

Angus glared at Rabbit with a look of pure disgust that distorted his handsome features.

"You shouldn't even eat with pigs, let alone in polite company!" he snapped. Then he marched out of the room.

Maybe he shouldn't, but *you* should! I thought to myself.

I didn't say anything out loud because poor Dora was upset enough already.

A few minutes later, Angus came back with another suitcoat on. He sat down and proceeded to eat a huge meal in outraged silence.

Phew! talk about a mean streak, I thought. Beside him, I'm as sweet as cotton candy.

When he'd finished eating, he suddenly glared at me and snapped, "I've never even *heard* of such a thing as a female veterinarian."

"You will!" I retorted immediately.

A pained expression crossed Dora's face, so I changed the subject.

"Where do you live in Toronto?" I asked in as friendly a tone as I could muster.

He dabbed at his perfect mouth daintily with the corner of his napkin before replying.

"I have excellent accommodation with a very refined family in the Beaches," he answered haughtily.

"Oh, I know where that is. We often have picnics down at Kew Beach. My family — my city family, that is — live in the east end, too. On Rose Avenue."

"Never heard of the place," Angus said huffily.

I don't know what would have come out of my mouth after that remark if fate hadn't intervened in the form of the train's warning whistle.

Angus had to run to catch it, his mother puffing behind him, lugging his heavy suitcase.

*   *   *

When Dora and I had finished the washing up, we all went into the parlour to listen to the gramophone. Rabbit wound it up and put on a record. Eddie Cantor began to sing "If you knew Susie like I know Susie."

Rabbit wiggled his ears in perfect time to the music. He didn't seem the least bit perturbed by what'd gone on earlier, and that really puzzled me.

Rabbit and Uncle Herb enjoyed an after-supper chaw. Then at the end of the third record, Uncle Herb said, "Well, I'd best be shoving off. It's darkening down and one of my headlamps is out."

He thanked Dora for the good grub and said goodbye. Then he and I walked hand in hand to the pickup.

"I don't understand, Uncle Herb," I said.

He chawed away and didn't answer.

"Angus is so different from either of his parents. He's so mean and disrespectful. Gosh, our Elmer is about Angus's age and my pa would knock him flat if he dared to talk to him like that."

Uncle Herb sent a jet of tobacco juice sailing over the pickup. We heard it splat on the other side.

Still he didn't say anything. He could be stubborn too when he felt like it.

"And another funny thing. I can't for the life of me figure out who's side Angus favours. He's not the least bit like his father, he's so darned handsome! No offence intended to Rabbit, of course."

"Climb up in the cab there, Maggie," interrupted Uncle Herb. "You choke and I'll crank."

It was the perfect foil. Uncle Herb knew how I loved to get my hands on the steering wheel.

He swung the crank around twice and the engine rumbled into life. I revved it up, then shoved over to make room for Uncle Herb behind the wheel. We sat there for a minute without speaking, jiggling with the rhythm of the motor.

Finally I could contain myself no longer.

"It's just that I feel sorry for Dora and Rabbit," I persisted. "Imagine having an only child as mean as that Angus."

Then at last Uncle Herb spoke.

"Well, Maggie, I reckon you're old enough to know. Roger Hare ain't the boy's real father. They're no kith or kin at all. But Rabbit's been a good father to Angus ever since the boy was knee-high to a grasshopper."

I was dumbfounded at the revelation.

"Who *is* his real father then?" I asked incredulously.

"Don't know. Never asked. Me and Mag figure it's none of our business."

He looked me straight in the eye when he said that and I knew he was warning me that it was none of mine either.

"I'll keep it under my hat," I promised.

Then I kissed him goodbye on his stubbly chin, hopped out of the cab and waved until the truck disappeared around the corner of Main and Rail streets.

* * *

That night, Rabbit went to bed early.

"Well, what did you think of my lad?" Dora asked, blind mother love shining from her eyes.

"He's handsome as all get out."

At least I could say that and mean it.

But in my mind I could hear my mother saying, "Handsome is as handsome does!"

"I'll bet he could get into pictures if he went to Hollywood," I continued.

Dora beamed at my praise. I should've left it at that, but my curiosity got the better of me again and I couldn't resist adding, "I can't help wondering who he looks like."

Dora held a spoonful of sugar very still over her tea. Instantly I wished with all my heart I'd kept my mouth shut.

Dora's voice was strangely quiet when she answered, "He gets his good looks from his pa. And his orneryness too."

I tried to cover up quickly.

"I sure know what it's like to inherit orneryness. Ma says I'm my Grandma Marshall all over. She had a mean streak a mile wide."

76

The more I said, the worse it got.

But to my relief, Dora just laughed. Then we spread the newspapers on the table, set out the breakfast dishes and went to bed too.

Angus's father was never mentioned again.

15
Fifth form high

When I began my senior year, I quickly found that everything — textbooks, teachers, friends — was new and exciting. Not only that, but in fifth form there were lots more boys than girls in the class. This was because senior year was preparation for college, and not many parents encouraged their girls to go to college. Times were hard. Some kids even had to drop out of school to help support their families.

If folks could afford to send one of their offspring to university at all, boys tended to get preference. After all, reasoned their parents, educating a girl was a waste of money in the long run, because girls only became housewives and mothers — or old maids. How much learning did you need for that?

I was one of the lucky few. Aunt Marg and Uncle Herb not only encouraged me, they put up the money when the time came — eighty-five dollars for every term! It sounded like a fortune, so I offered to help by getting an after-school job. Uncle Herb turned thumbs down on that idea.

"You're my right-hand man on the farm, Maggie. Ain't nobody deserves an eddication more'n you do."

*   *   *

The problem was, not everybody agreed with him.

For instance, our principal and science teacher, Mr. Bannister, was dead set against higher education for women. Every time I raised my hand to answer a question, he'd look right through me and ask the boy behind me.

"I just know I'm going to lose my temper and tell him off, Dora," I complained one day after a particularly humiliating experience. "And if I do, I'll be in trouble for sure. Once my tongue gets loose, there's no telling what might come out of my mouth. Even I don't know until it's too late."

Dora was rocking briskly to and fro as she knitted a red woollen square. She was making an afghan this time.

"Why don't you try a new tack then?" she suggested.

"Like what?"

I sat down at the table, opened my excercise book, sucked the oil off my new pen-nib and dipped it in the inkpot.

"Just pay him no mind, Meggie, no mind at all. Don't even give him the time of day."

She squinted through her downstairs glasses and picked up a dropped stitch.

"Just you do your level best on your own. Then when exam time comes, he'll get his comeuppance and you'll earn an extra feather in your cap."

Dora chuckled as she rolled up her skein of yarn and spiked her needles through it.

"He's an old-fashioned stick, and that's a fact. Why, he didn't even approve of women getting the vote in 1920. Said the Lord never intended the female mind to deal in politics. But for all that, he's not a mean man, Meggie. Just ignorant. There's a world of difference."

She wagged her finger at me to make her point.

"There's a good side to Dusty Bannister," she continued while she filled the kettle. "I should know. He sure stood by me when I was left alone with Angus. Wouldn't hear a word against me. And he took care of his widowed mother to her dying day. Fair worshipped the woman, he did. That says a lot for a man."

"Dusty! What a cute name!" I laughed. "Why do you call Mr. Bannister that?"

"Oh, it goes way back to our schooldays. His real name is Durward. Well, no matter how clean and paid for Durward got sent off to school, he'd scuff his feet along the dirt road and arrive at the schoolhouse door covered in dust. Then the schoolmarm — Miss Teasey was her name — would make him jump up and down and shake himself off before she'd let him in the classroom. So that's how he came by his nickname. He'll always be dusty to me."

From that day on, every time I looked at scowling Mr. Bannister I'd get a picture in my mind's eye of the dusty little boy he used to be, and somehow that softened my feelings towards him.

After all, I wasn't so prim and proper myself. My favourite get-up even at the age of sixteen was still my overalls, especially when they smelled rich and horsey.

* * *

I made a brand-new friend in fifth form. Her name was Phylis Carpenter and she lived across town.

Her folks had just moved to Shelburne from Orange-ville.

Phylis and I hit it off right away because we were so much alike. Not only were we similar in personality, but we were also both tall and skinny with dark curly hair and freckles. The only difference was that Phyllis didn't wear spectacles.

"My brother Willard says I'm mean as a skunk," Phylis confided cheerfully as we sat on the girls' side of the school steps eating our mashed potato sandwiches.

When I heard that, I told her then and there all about the nasty streak I'd inherited from my Grandma Marshall.

"I practically hate Willard," she said, blowing up her lunch bag and bursting it with a loud bang. "You know why?"

"No, why?"

"Because the other day I was in the kitchen when he came in the front hall with a boy named Bert Stromberg. Do you know Bert Stromberg?"

"Oh, you mean Philbert the nut," I replied maliciously.

Bert had had to repeat fifth form because he'd failed last year. Served him right, I thought, for wasting his time lollygagging after Belinda.

"Sure, I've seen him around."

"Well, they didn't know I was home.

"I heard Bert say, 'I hear you've got a sister. What's she like?'

"Then that rotten brother of mine said, 'Oh, you mean old freckle-face. You wouldn't be interested in her. She's as mean as a weasel, and she's got a figure like a tableleg.'

"It was that last remark that made me see red,

so I bounded through the kitchen door and surprised the lights out of them.

"Well, at least Bert had the decency to blush, but that rat Willard laughed his head off and said, 'See what I mean?'

"So I screeched at him, 'While you're at it, did you tell him you still have to have a rubber sheet on your bed, and that you're a typhoid carrier?'"

I almost choked on a crust and Phylis had to thump me on the back to save my life.

Phylis was a barrel of fun. We got on like a house afire. The only problem was Eva. I knew she was jealous of Phylis and I hated to hurt her feelings. I still considered Eva and Matt my best friends, but Eva was boring compared to Phylis, so I was torn between the two.

16
Help!

The *CRASH* could be heard for miles around.

Eva said Mrs. Stromberg woke up screaming that the world was coming to an end. And Phylis Carpenter, whose house was on the outskirts of town, said she was sure her roof was going to cave in. So you can imagine how it sounded to *us* — because our roof *did* cave in.

I woke with a shock to find myself trapped under the collapsed ceiling. Only the sturdy iron bedstead posts had saved me from being crushed flat as a pancake. As Rabbit said later, by rights I should've been killed.

The horrendous crash still echoing in my ears, I began to scream. I'd been sleeping on my stomach, so I turned my head sideways — and saw what looked like a huge, craggy arm in a tattered sleeve poking through the broken beams. Giant, shadowy fingers seemed to be snatching at my hair.

"Dora! Dora!" I shrieked at the top of my lungs. But my voice was drowned out by the sound of grinding metal and groaning rafters and a strange assortment of noises coming from outdoors — loud shouts and wild hysterical cries.

"Meggie!" Dora screamed. "Are you alive?"

"I think so," I yelled back. "But I'm trapped in my bed. What happened?"

"Train got wrecked . . . jack-knifed right behind the house . . . split the old elm tree . . . cattle car's smashed to smithereens."

"*That's* what I can hear. It's the cows. I'm scared, Dora."

"Rabbit's gone for help, Meggie. Don't move a muscle."

I tried not to, but I was shaking from head to toe by now and bits of wood and plaster kept falling all around me. Then as my eyes adjusted to the moonlight slanting through the broken roof, I saw to my relief that the craggy arm was a limb from the elm tree in the Hare's yard, and the phantom fingers were autumn leaves plucking at my hair.

At last I heard Rabbit's voice.

"Meggie!" he called. "What's grey and wrinkled and carries a trunk?"

That Rabbit, I thought, he'll be asking riddles at Armageddon.

"An old grey mouse going on holidays," I answered, trying not to laugh.

Then I heard Rabbit say, "She'll be all right, that one. Now hang on, Meg, and we'll get you outta there afore you can spell Jack Robinson."

"Please, God, help!" I prayed fervently.

Then I heard a man's voice saying, "We'll prop the wall up with our backs while you get her out."

The voice sounded familiar, but at that moment I didn't know or care who it was.

"I've got ahold of you, girl."

Suddenly Rabbit had a tight grip on my ankles.

"You'll have to wiggle out on your belly. There ain't no room to turn over."

I started squirming backwards as Rabbit pulled me by the feet. My long legs scraped over the iron bedrail.

Glancing quickly over my shoulder to check my progress, I saw in the moonlight two pale mounds.

Oh, no! My behind! My bare behind! My nightdress had worked its way up to my waist, leaving my bottom naked as a jay bird.

"Rabbit! Stop! My nightdress!"

Then I heard Dora's fierce voice.

"You men, shut your eyes or I'll blind you with a red-hot poker."

"Yes, ma'am!" I heard them answer.

Minutes dragged by like hours as I worked my way backwards.

The combination of the huge branch and the collapsed wall trying to close in on me gave me a horrible, stifling feeling.

"Talk to me, Dora," I begged.

So she did. Over and over again she assured me that everything was going to be all right.

Suddenly there came a grinding, rending CRACK, and the wall shifted ominously.

Grunting and straining, one of the men holding up the wall gasped, "Hurry up before our backs give out."

"Meggie," Rabbit's tone was dead serious now, "our eyes is all shut and Dora's got a quilt ready to throw over you, so wiggle outta there before the whole dern place falls in."

I made one last desperate effort — and all of a sudden I was free.

Dora wrapped the quilt around me and led me downstairs.

Just as we got to the parlour door, there was another big *CRASH*.

"Roger!" Dora screamed.

"We're right behind you. Everything's under control."

The electricity had been knocked out, so Dora lit the oil lamp she kept for emergencies.

I was still shaking like a leaf as my rescuers came in through the kitchen doorway covered in plaster dust. In the flickering lamplight they looked like three ghostly apparitions. Then they went outside to check the damage.

Oddly, not a thing had been disturbed in the kitchen. Not even a pan had fallen off the wall. Dora shut both doors and I felt safe at last.

"Dora," my voice was still a bit shaky, "who were those men with Rabbit?"

"You didn't recognize them? Mr. Stromberg and Philbert."

Bert! Oh, how I wished I'd died!

"Dora, do you think they saw?"

"Saw what?"

She filled the kettle and put it on to boil.

"You know."

Dora said nothing. Instead, she silently fetched the speckled teapot from the cupboard. The white enamel mugs were already on the table for breakfast.

"My *derrière!*" I yelled at last, almost in tears.

"What's a *derrière?* I never heard tell of such a thing," she hedged innocently.

"Well then, my naked bottom. You know what that is, don't you?" I was getting mad.

Her back was to me, her salt-and-pepper braid swinging at her waist.

Then I noticed her shoulders jiggling. She was laughing! The silly article was laughing at me.

"Dora! How can you laugh. I nearly get killed, and lose all my dignity in the process, and you stand there guffawing."

She swilled hot water in the teapot and dumped it down the sink.

"Margaret, my dear, we'll probably never know who saw what. Just thank your lucky stars that their backs were strong enough to hold the wall up."

She began to mash the tea.

"That's all right for you to say," I grumbled, "but I'll be plagued by it for the rest of my natural life."

"Well if you are, my girl" — she poured strong, steaming brew into our mugs — "then more fool you!"

* * *

The train wreck and my miraculous escape were the talk of the town, but no one snickered when they saw me, and no rude remarks were ever made, so I knew that Bert had had the decency to keep his mouth shut. Either that, or the threat of Dora's red-hot poker had scared the daylights out of him.

Anyway, when I met him on Main Street a few days later, all he said was, "Are you okay, Marg?"

I'll always be grateful to him for that.

17
Opportunity knocks

My bedchamber was the only room in the house that was completely demolished, so I went back to the farm until Rabbit rebuilt it.

Uncle Herb took me in to school each day. One crispy, autumn morning as we were driving through a shower of falling leaves, I had an inspiration.

"Uncle Herb," I said, "why don't I drive myself in. Then you wouldn't have to be bothered."

"Because you ain't got no licence."

"Neither have you."

"That's different."

"Why?"

" 'Cause I'm a growed man."

"Well how do I get a licence, then?"

"You got to take a driving test in Barrie. But first you got to have lots of practice."

"Then this is my chance. If you let me drive back and forth every day, I'll soon have lots of practice. Besides, I've already practised in our lane. I can back up and change gears and stop on a dime."

That last bit was an exaggeration. The brakes of the pickup were so bad I had to stand up on them to make them work.

Uncle Herb looked pretty skeptical.

"I got a feeling Mag ain't going to like it," he said.

"Well let's not tell her until I'm ready to try my test. Then if I pass and she agrees, will you let me drive myself to school?"

"I'll think on it," he hedged.

Rolling down the window, he let a stream of tobacco juice fly with the leaves.

"I don't see how we could keep Mag from getting wind of it. More'n likely some busybody would see us and spill the beans."

"We'll leave early and take the back roads. That old road north of Potter's place is hardly ever used any more. And Mr. Potter couldn't tell if he wanted to, because he's blind as a bat."

"By rights we should discuss it with your aunt first," Uncle Herb said.

But I could feel him weakening, so I persisted.

"Let's keep her in the dark until I'm ready to try my test. Then we'll surprise her. Is it a deal?"

After chawing and spitting and contemplating for about five more minutes, Uncle Herb finally nodded and we shook on it. I think he secretly got a kick out of the idea of trying to put one over on Aunt Marg because it was so darn hard to do.

Every day for a month we took Potter's old road with me at the wheel. I clashed gears and made the truck leapfrog up hills, and stalled it about a dozen times. And every time I stalled it, Uncle Herb made me get out and crank.

It was hard work, cranking, but he insisted that if I was going to be a driver I had to know how.

I was improving every day and getting as confident as all get out when I had my first accident.

A hedgehog ran across my path and I swerved

violently to miss it — and landed us in the ditch. We were both shaken up, but not really hurt.

"I'm sorry, Uncle Herb," I said, fearful that I'd ruined my chances. "What should I have done?"

"Well, Maggie," he rubbed his head where it'd bumped on the roof, "in a case like that, it's either him or us. Just think what might've happened if we were on a busy highway and you'd swung out into the path of another veehickle."

I twisted my neck to get the crick out of it.

"I won't do it again," I promised.

We climbed out of the truck to survey the situation. As luck would have, right at that moment along came Barney Slinger in his tow truck.

When he saw us, he rolled his cab window down and hollered, "What in blazes are you two doing out in this neck of the woods, Herb?"

Then Uncle Herb said the strangest thing.

"I'm fine Barney," he replied. "How's yourself?"

We both looked curiously at Uncle Herb, then I jumped into the breach.

"I'm learning to drive, Mr. Slinger," I explained.

Barney laughed and said, "You're supposed to drive on the road. Need any help?"

It was a joke, not a question.

"You're lucky I took this short cut today or you'd be walking into town. You'd never drive outta there."

He hopped out, inspected the depth of the ditch, hooked us up and towed us out in no time flat, simple as that. Uncle Herb tried to pay him for his trouble, but Barney wouldn't hear of it.

"What's neighbours for?" he said. "But you better be more careful, Maggie. You two could've got banged up pretty bad. Or worse yet, broke an axle."

"I know," I answered ruefully. "But, Mr. Slinger, could I ask you one more favour?"

"Depends on how much time it'll take. I'm a busy man."

"Oh, it won't take any time at all," I assured him. "I just want to ask you to promise not to tell anybody about my driving lessons so it doesn't spoil the surprise for Aunt Marg."

He laughed when he heard that.

"I'd like to be a mouse in the corner when you surprise her. You can count on me."

He twisted his thumb and finger across his mouth three times.

"My lips are buttoned up."

By the time another couple of weeks had gone by, I was nearly an expert, so I asked Uncle Herb if I was ready.

"Ready as you'll ever be, Maggie," was his reply. "Now all we got to worry about is telling your aunt."

That night after supper we confessed.

"Herbert Alfred Wilkinson!"

Aunt Marg was furious.

"You did what? You taught our Margaret how to drive. You did that behind my back?"

"I had no choice, Meg. She made me do it, didn't you, Maggie?"

"Made you, indeed!"

She didn't give me a chance to defend him.

"You both deserve a good hiding."

"Shall I find a switch, Aunt Marg?" cried Gracie gleefully.

Gracie wasn't too thrilled about sharing her bed

with me again, so she wasn't sorry to see me in trouble, even if it did include her beloved uncle.

"Oh, Aunt Marg," I pleaded, grabbing her hand. "Come for a ride with me and let me prove how good I am."

"Good or bad has nothing to do with it, Margaret. It's just the idea that the two of you would deceive me."

"We're truly sorry, aren't we, Uncle Herb?"

Uncle Herb nodded his fuzzy red head vigorously.

"C'mon, Aunt Marg."

I got her coat down from the hook on the door and held it out for her.

She gave a short, impatient huff and shrugged into it. Reluctantly, she climbed into the cab of the truck. Uncle Herb had already started the engine, so I threw it in gear and took off. I drove for about five miles with the utmost care. Aunt Marg didn't say a word until I'd glided to a smooth stop back in the barnyard.

I glanced at her anxiously. To my relief I saw she was smiling. In fact she was grinning from ear to ear.

"You drive just like me!" she declared proudly. "We'll go straight into Barrie tomorrow."

We took the car instead of the pickup because it had better brakes.

I could've passed that test with one hand tied behind my back.

"You're a pretty good driver for a girl," the tester had to admit.

"You're a pretty good tester for a boy!" I retorted.

I was glad I had my licence safely in hand before I said that, because it made him mad as hops.

For the next month I drove myself triumphantly to and from school in Shelburne.

Aunt Marg laid down some hard and fast rules: no boys in the car except Matt — what a pain that was, but I'd have agreed to anything for the privilege of driving. No speeding — twenty miles an hour was my limit. And keep both hands firmly on the steering wheel.

Eva was my daily passenger. At first, Jessie didn't take to the idea of two girls driving alone back and forth on country roads. What if we ran into problems? The car might develop engine trouble or blow a tire. But Matt assured his mother that I could handle such emergencies as well as he could. I was pleased as punch when he said that! And Zach said it would be mighty fine having Eva home every night for a change, so Jessie finally relented.

"Isn't it wonderful, Marg. Just the two of us again," remarked Eva as we bounced along the bumpy side road to Shelburne.

I knew what she meant. We hardly ever saw each other alone any more because Phylis was always there.

And it *was* wonderful. It made me appreciate Eva's genuine loyalty and her quiet intelligence. Phylis was fun — she was always saying goofy things to make me laugh — but if I ever had to choose between them, there'd be no contest. Eva would win hands down.

And of course I was the envy of my schoolmates. After all, who else had an almost brand new Model A Ford to park beside Mr. Bannister's Whippet in the schoolyard?

18
My dear uncle

One night while I was doing my physics homework by the white light of the Coleman lamp and Aunt Marg was recording the day's events in her journal, we heard sleet pinging on the windowpane.

Aunt Marg got up and peered out between cupped hands.

"I think it'll be risky driving tomorrow, Margaret," she said anxiously. "The piazza steps are already coated in ice."

Uncle Herb folded his newspaper.

"What's that you said, Mag?" he asked. So she repeated her forecast.

"Mebbe I'd better run you and Eva into school tomorrow, Maggie," he suggested.

My instant protest was drowned out by the jangling of the telephone.

"For mercy sakes, who could that be at this hour?" wondered Aunt Marg. "Answer it, will you, Herb?"

"Can't! No time."

He jumped up as quick as a jack-in-the-box.

"I got chores to do in the barn."

Grabbing his coat and cap from the doorhook, he high-tailed it out through the woodshed.

The telephone rang again — two longs and two shorts.

"I'll get it," I said.

I lifted the receiver and tilted the flared mouthpiece at the bottom of the box up to my mouth. I was now so much taller than Aunt Marg that we couldn't talk on the same level.

It was Dora on the phone telling me in an animated voice that my room was ready. Her excitement was contagious, so I promised that I'd come the very next day.

Rabbit had forbidden me to set foot in their house after the catastrophe — because, he explained, he wanted to surprise me.

Well, did he ever! The room was brand new, not just Angus's old room done over, but brand, spanking new.

Rabbit had installed a bay window with a hinged window seat that you could sit on and store things in, and he'd lined the walls with flawless pine.

Dora had sewn blue dotted swiss curtains and a matching counterpane.

To top it all off, they'd bought a new bed and washstand from the Eaton's catalogue. The washstand had a pink china pitcher in a matching bowl on top, and an oval looking glass that could be tipped to any angle. A pink chamber pot was hidden behind a door lower down.

The crowning glory was a bearskin rug beside my bed. Now I wouldn't have to step out onto cold linoleum!

"Well, Meg?"

Dora was all atwitter, waiting for my reaction.

"Out with it! What've you got to say?"

For once in my life, I was almost speechless.

"It's a dream come true, Dora," I managed at last. "I've always wanted a room like this."

"Oh, and just you wait 'til you see the closet!" she cried.

She flung open the door of a new corner wardrobe. "There's room enough for all your things in here, even your winter coat. You won't have to hang it on that old hall tree any more. It'll hold its shape lots better on a clothes hanger."

"That reminds me, Meggie."

Rabbit had been leaning on the doorjamb, silently taking it all in. He hadn't said a word, but his ears and nose were wiggling a mile a minute, so I knew there was a riddle coming on.

"What kind of coat do you put on wet?"

Quick as a wink I answered, "A coat of paint!"

"Shoot!" he hooted.

Then he gave his knee a slap and went clumping down the stairs laughing his head off . . .

That night, Dora prepared a special welcome-home supper and served it on the tablecloth. There were potato pancakes, fried turnips, stuffed baked rabbit, and apple pie.

After supper, Rabbit started singing in his funny nasal voice, *"Leave the dishes in the sink, Ma.*

"Leave the dishes in the sink.

"Each dirty plate will have to wait.

"Tonight we're going to celebrate.

"So, leave the dishes in the sink!"

"That's a dandy idea," laughed Dora. "And just like the fine folk that we are, we'll take our tea in the parlour."

The parlour had also changed a lot since the last time I'd been in it. It wasn't cluttered any more with Dora's precious gewgaws because they'd nearly all been smashed in the catastrophe.

And something else was different. Rabbit had traded in his gramophone for a brand-new electric radio. It had eight tubes, he said, and he could tune in at least four stations — five on a good night — just as clear as if they were coming from down on Main Street.

That night, we listened to a marvelous story called *The General Died at Dawn*. Dora and I sat spellbound, but halfway through it Rabbit stretched and yawned and said he was going to hit the hay. Dora and I stayed glued to the radio until the final awful moment when the general passed bravely away on the new Philco.

Then, sighing with sad satisfaction, we went into the kitchen to do the washing up and have our bedtime repast.

"How come Rabbit went to bed in the middle of such a swell story, Dora?" I asked, really mystified.

"Well, Meggie, just between you, me and the lamppost," she paused, mashed the tea and poured it through a sieve into our cups, "my Roger's got his good points" — she always referred to her husband by his correct name when she was being serious — "but a long attention span isn't one of them. He gets restless quicker than you and me."

We were just polishing off the last of the pie when the telephone rang.

"Who in the world could that be calling at this hour?" declared Dora, sounding just like Aunt Marg. "You get it like a good scout, will you, Meg?"

It was Aunt Marg.

"How d'you like your new bed chamber, Margaret?" she asked excitedly.

"It's just gorgeous, Aunt Marg. I can't wait 'til you see it."

"Well, Dora gave me a sneak preview a week ago, so I couldn't wait to hear what you had to say. By the way, your father phoned tonight."

"He did!"

Instantly I saw my pa in my mind's eye, tall and lanky, black curly hair like mine and big dark eyes behind thick horn-rimmed spectacles.

"What did Pa want, Aunt Marg?"

Cold shivers ran over my skin at the thought of anything wrong at home.

"He wanted to speak to you, but I told him you were back in Shelburne."

"Why did he want to speak to me especially?"

The hair on the back of my neck prickled with anxiety.

"Oh, he was just checking to see if you'd suffered any ill effects to your nerves after what you went through in the catastrophe. I assured him you were fine and dandy."

I felt a wave of relief, then a backwash of disappointment.

"I wish I'd been there," I said.

"Well, never mind, dear. I promised him you'd phone home on the weekend. Then I had a chat with your mother. She sends her love and says to tell you they're all in the pink."

"Thanks, Aunt Marg. Can I speak to Uncle Herb for a minute?"

I heard her call him from wherever he was.

"Your uncle says he's too tuckered to talk, Margaret, but Gracie's pestering at my elbow, so I'll put her on. Good night, love."

"Good night, Aunt Marg. Tell Uncle Herb good night."

I talked to Gracie for a while, but it *was* long distance, so I rang off before too much time went by.

I hung up slowly, a feeling of apprehension creeping over me. Dora stood in the doorway, arms folded, a look of consternation puckering her brow. She'd overheard enough of the conversation to put two and two together.

"It's not like Uncle Herb," I said, following her back to the kitchen. "He always wants to talk to me. I hope Gracie hasn't completely replaced me in his affections."

"No, no, Meggie. Herb's not like that. He's got his faults, but his heart's as big as all outdoors. There's plenty of room for the both of you, and some to spare."

"Well, why the heck wouldn't he talk to me, then?"

"Maybe he's sick, Meg, and just won't let on. Remember last winter when Roger had the quincy and he wouldn't admit it until he was flat on his back?"

"No, Uncle Herb's not sick."

I was sure of that because I knew Aunt Marg would've said something. You couldn't pull the wool over her eyes where sickness was concerned. I'd tried it often enough myself. Something else was nagging at me.

Suddenly I knew.

"He can't hear well on the telephone any more, Dora. He runs a mile every time the phone rings. Come to think of it, he doesn't hear anything like he used to."

Then I told her about Barney Slinger's question

when he found us in the ditch and Uncle Herb's strange answer.

"Matter of fact, I quizzed him about it later and he said if folks would stop mumbling and speak up he'd hear them just fine."

We sat silently at the kitchen table finishing our tea.

"Dora," I just had to say it out loud, "I think Uncle Herb's going deaf."

With downcast eyes she absently wet her finger on her tongue and dabbed at the crumbs on the table.

"Well, don't fret yourself until he's seen Dr. Tom, Meggie," she said. "He'll know what to do."

I decided to discuss it with Aunt Marg on the weekend. But the very next day, something unexpected happened that sent me flying home.

19
Chip off the old block

"Peggy!" Gracie screamed hysterically into the telephone.

My heart gave a wild thump.

"What is it, Gracie?"

I was terrified of the answer. Visions of Aunt Marg lying stricken on the floor or Uncle Herb pinned helplessly under the tractor out in the field flashed through my mind.

"It's a fawn! A baby deer! It's all tore open and bleeding. Uncle Herb carried it into the house and wrapped it in flannel, but now we don't know what else to do."

"Call the vet!" I shouted into the mouthpiece.

"He doesn't answer."

"Where's Aunt Marg?"

"She's at Delmer Dandy's. Clarrisa Dandy took a bad turn yesterday, so Aunt Marg said she'd stay all night. They haven't got a phone. Please, Peg, please come home!"

Suddenly I was very calm.

"Is the fawn still bleeding?"

"I think so. The flannel's all soaked."

"Tell Uncle Herb I have to speak to him."

She told him and I heard him say, "There's been

enough talk. Tell Maggie I'm on my way in to get her."

"Gracie, listen to me carefully."

"I am, Peg."

Her voice was a fearful, childish whisper.

"Get some towels. Fold them into a big pad and press down firmly on the wound. Talk to the fawn softly to keep him quiet."

I hung up and looked at Dora.

"Will you come with me, Dora?" I asked as I climbed into my overalls.

In answer, she got my bag out of the closet. Over the years I'd put together a doctoring kit like Aunt Marg's — disinfectants, wads of cotton and rolls of gauze, a razor-sharp knife, long pointed tweezers, needles and thread.

"I'll just leave Rabbit a note pinned to the kitchen curtains where he'll be sure to see it," she said.

Oh, how I wished I'd driven the car in. But Aunt Marg had needed it because she'd several patients she had to see.

By the time Uncle Herb came racing down Rail Street, Dora and I were waiting impatiently at the door.

We made it back to Green Meadows in record time. Uncle Herb flew along the bumpy roads at forty miles an hour.

I leapt out of the pickup before it came to a full stop and ran with my bag into the house.

There sat Gracie on the floor, her round face smeared with blood and tears. Dark brown blood was drying on her chubby outspread fingers.

"Oh, Peg," she looked at me with swimming, tragic eyes, "I think I've let her die."

The long-legged little creature lay perfectly still. I snatched the looking glass off the wall above the washbench and held it close to the fawn's mouth and nostrils.

Slowly a patch of mist appeared.

"She's alive!" I cried. "Dora, you help Gracie while I scrub my hands. Uncle Herb, I'll need more light."

They followed my orders like soldiers.

Cautiously I lifted the blood-soaked pad, expecting to have to deal with a sudden red jet, but none came.

"The bleeding's stopped," I sighed. "Now all I have to do is patch the wound up."

It wasn't as easy as it sounded. There was a terrible, jagged hole, big enough to bury my fist in. I could see vital organs laid bare, but miraculously the main blood vessel hadn't been severed. I could actually see the artery pulsing as the fawn's lifeblood ran through it.

Using the tweezers, I began picking out bits of rusty metal and strands of twisted steel.

A barbed wire fence, I thought. She got caught in a barbed wire fence and tore herself free.

Then I spied something that made my blood boil — a tiny lead slug buried in her flesh.

A bullet!

I knew it was hunting season, but what kind of sportsman would shoot at a baby deer? Apart from anything else, it was against the law.

Watching intently over my shoulder, Uncle Herb said gravely, "I'll take care of that, Maggie."

I grasped the slug with the tweezers and nipped it out clean as a whistle and dropped it into Uncle Herb's hand.

Blood spurted and I staunched the flow with a wad of cotton.

When I was finally satisfied that I'd taken out every last piece of foreign matter, I carefully sponged the area with disinfectant while Dora sterilized a needle and thread.

I tried to pull the skin together with my thumb and finger, but the torn edges wouldn't fit.

"Boil the scissors from Aunt Marg's work basket, will you, Dora?"

The little animal began to stir.

"Quickly, Gracie! Get the bottle of chloroform from my bag."

Uncle Herb handed her a clean handkerchief folded into a square pad.

"Put a few drops on it, Gracie. Then be ready to give her a whiff."

Gracie carried out my instructions like a veteran.

After what seemed like ages, the scissors were sterilized and cool enough for me to handle. I snipped the ragged skin away and pulled the edges neatly together. Then I took my first stitch.

Suddenly the fawn stirred again and opened its eyes. They were large as saucers and dark as midnight — and filled with terror. Bleating a wild, terrified cry, she began to struggle.

Uncle Herb dropped to his knees and pinned her front legs down while Dora grabbed the flailing back ones. Gracie, without being told, hugged the head tight to her body and administered more chloroform.

Slowly the little beast relaxed and lay still. I worked as fast as I could, stitching and knotting, stitching and knotting the same way I'd seen Doc Wiley do on a wounded dog once.

At last the gaping hole was closed. I'd sewn a nice, neat seam shaped like a wedge of pie.

Uncle Herb got an old quilt from the cupboard.

"Easy does it," he said as all four of us helped lift the sleeping baby onto the clean bedding.

Then he wrapped the bloody flannel in newspapers while Dora hunted up Aunt Marg's pail and string mop and went to work on the stained floorboards. We'd hardly glanced at each other throughout the whole ordeal. I turned to tell Gracie how brave she'd been, only to see hero worship glowing from her big green eyes.

"You did it, Peg!" she said in an awe-struck whisper. "You saved the fawn's life."

"Not me, Gracie," I smiled at her, smoothing her dishevelled red hair behind her shoulders. "*You* did. If you hadn't controlled the bleeding, the little creature would've been dead long before I got here."

"Really, Peg? You're not just saying that?"

"Really," I nodded solemnly. "And since you saved her life, she belongs to you. That's the rule isn't it, Uncle Herb?"

"Yep. Them's the rules, petootie," he said as he pinched Gracie's round cheek. "It'll be up to you to take care of her until she's strong enough to go free."

He knelt and examined the V-shaped gash.

"By that time, it'll be dead of winter," he murmured anxiously. "She'll never survive out there in the bush at that time of year."

His words made Gracie gasp. Then her face lit up with an idea.

"We can keep her in the barn until spring.

She'll be my pet, like Starr is Peggy's pet. Is there enough hay to feed one more animal, Uncle Herb?"

"More than enough," he replied. "But deer don't eat hay like horses, petootie. It cramps them up and gives them the scours. No, she'll have to have corn and cedar."

"Where'll we get corn and cedar?" worried Gracie.

"We can buy corn from the feed store in Shelburne, and we can bring cedar boughs in from the bush. They got to be fresh every day."

"I'll get the cedar, Uncle Herb," volunteered Gracie.

"No, Gracie, you ain't to go near the bush by your ownself. You might get turned around and get lost. Don't you worry your head about the cedar. I'll take care of that chore. Now you and Maggie go wash yourselves. It's a messy job being a vet."

After we'd tidied up and Dora had put the kitchen back to rights, we all squatted on our haunches around the groggy fawn, stroking and comforting her. The glossy reddish-brown coat shimmered under our touch.

At last the curled eyelashes fluttered open, and this time she stayed quite calm.

Just at that crucial moment when we were winning the fawn's confidence, who should come bustling in the door but Aunt Marg.

"Well, for land's sake," she cried, dropping her bag with a thud on the floor. "What are you doing home, Margaret? And what in the world are you all on your knees for?"

The fawn jerked and bleated pitifully.

"Hush!" we all said at once.

When Aunt Marg saw what lay on the blanket,

she knelt down between Gracie and me and whispered, "What happened?"

In a breathless voice, Gracie told her all about it.

Gingerly Aunt Marg lifted the gauze padding and peered at the stitchwork.

"You did this, Margaret?" she asked in an admiring whisper.

"Yes, Aunt Marg. But Gracie deserves the credit. She's a real trooper."

Then Dora piped up, "She's a chip off the old block, if you want my opinion."

"What block?" asked Gracie curiously.

"This one right here."

Uncle Herb put his arm around my shoulders.

"It looks to me like we got two up-and-coming vets in this here family, Mag."

Turning to Gracie, Aunt Marg gave her a fierce hug and covered her beaming face with kisses.

"I'm ever so proud of you, old sweetheart," she declared.

We were pleased as punch with ourselves, Gracie and me. Especially me. It was the first time since my little sister had come to live with us that I hadn't felt the slightest twinge of jealousy when Aunt Marg called Gracie by my special pet name.

Maybe, just maybe, I was growing up at last.

20
The culprit

Uncle Herb lost no time in ferreting out the culprit who'd shot Petunia, as Gracie called the little creature.

First he made inquiries of all our neighbours for miles around. He took a notepad with him and a pencil stub that he licked before each entry. Then he wrote down everything they said.

He tracked down every clue like a detective, checking out every strange car in the area that day and finding out the name of every person who'd been seen carrying a gun.

Bit by bit, he sifted through the evidence until he'd narrowed it down to two possible suspects. One of the two had an airtight alibi.

The other was Matt.

"Well, Matt didn't do it," I said with finality.

"It's probably just hearsay," agreed Aunt Marg.

"I'm sorry to have to put the kibosh on that surmise, but I've got a mighty reliable witness. And you know how that boy loves to hunt. He's been toting a gun around these parts ever since Collie was a pup."

"But he wouldn't shoot a baby deer," I insisted.

Uncle Herb continued as if I hadn't spoken.

"He was seen on old Joe Boyle's place, and

that's where I found the fawn. Do you remember old Joe Boyle, Maggie?"

"Sure I do. He was that squatter that shot himself."

"That's the fella," agreed Uncle Herb. "And his shack's been deserted ever since. The barbed fence was down and gone to wrack and ruin and the fawn was all tangled up in the rusty wire. I had a deuce of a time cutting her loose 'cause she was wild with fear and pain."

He shook his head sadly, then continued.

"Harry Potter says he saw Matt prowling around old Joe Boyle's place that very day."

"Well, that doesn't prove anything. Old man Potter is potty anyway. And he's probably lying his head off."

"Harry's not potty, Maggie, and he ain't a liar," said Uncle Herb sharply.

"Well, Matt didn't do it!"

I banged my fist so hard on the table that the spoon glass jumped about two inches.

"And all we have to do to settle it is to ask Matt. He *never* lies."

I went straight to the telephone then and turned the crank. Nora Wiggins came on instantly.

"Central here!" she answered in her operator's voice.

"Nora, it's me, Margaret. Put me through to Briarwood Farm right away, please."

"Hmph!" she snorted as she rang the Muggins' phone. Nora didn't much appreciate a straight connection with no chit-chat.

She came back on the line.

"There's no answer," she reported triumphantly.

"There has to be," I insisted, almost angrily.

"Well, don't get your shirt in a knot. I'll try again."

I heard the telephone ringing off the hook, but there was still no answer.

"Are you sure you've got the right number? One long and two short?" I demanded.

"Now don't you go getting uppity with me, Margaret Rose Emerson. I know my job."

"Well, where the heck is everybody then?"

"How should I know?" Nora snapped. "I'm a telephone operator — and a good one, I might add — not a mind reader."

"Oh, gosh, Nora, I'm sorry. I'm all upset. I didn't mean to take it out on you. But I absolutely have to get in touch with Matt. I think I'll go over to Briarwood myself."

"Well, if there's anything I can do, Margaret" — my apology seemed to mollify her a bit — "just let me . . .

I rang off right in the middle of her sentence.

Aunt Marg knew I'd hung up on Nora because she knew Nora would be dying of curiosity. Being 'Central' for twenty years had made her that way. And she was a font of information too. Anything you wanted to know, you just had to ask Nora.

"Margaret," Aunt Marg reprimanded me. "That's no way to treat Nora, hanging up in her ear. She's a good scout and she's handled many an emergency. Just you wait until the next time you need her."

"I mind the time Nora saved the schoolhouse from burning to the ground," Uncle Herb said. "If she hadn't noticed the chimney fire in time, the whole shebang would've gone up in smoke. Lives might even have been lost. We'd be in a fine pickle without Nora, and that's a fact. We'll rue the day the telephone company replaces her with one of them modern switchboards."

"Nora's nice," put in Gracie as she brushed Silky's hair backwards, trying to make him look like a Persian. "She always gives me licorice roots."

"Nora! Nora! Nora!" I snapped, exasperated. "Where's Matt? That's what I want to know."

I already had my coat on.

"Can I have the keys to the truck, Uncle Herb?"

"Truck's got two flat tires, Maggie," said Uncle Herb.

"How about the car, Aunt Marg?"

"It's up on blocks in the driving shed for the winter. You know that, Margaret."

"I forgot," I sighed. "Well, I know one sure-fire way of getting there."

I didn't have to ask permission to ride Starr anymore. It went without saying. He was mine.

I was out the door in two shakes of a lamb's tail, or maybe Petunia's little powder puff.

Then, just as Starr and I were setting off down our lane, up the road came the Muggins' horse and buggy with the whole family squeezed in on the seat.

We pulled up side by side.

"Where you off to, girl?" asked Zacharia.

"I was on my way over to your place."

Zacharia waved towards the house and I turned Starr around and took him back to his stall. He stomped his front hoofs and grumbled in his throat the way horses do when they're mad, so I took the time to give him some extra oats.

"I'll be back soon," I promised when I'd finished

filling his bin — and quickly made a beeline for the house.

The second I saw all the long faces inside, I knew something was wrong. Jessie and Aunt Marg were sitting on the settle together looking agitated. Uncle Herb and Zach were muttering under their breath and Eva was standing beside Matt, her hand on his arm protectively.

As for Matt, well his hang-dog expression gave him away instantly — and Grandma Marshall's legacy started boiling in my veins.

I raced across the room and stopped right in front of him.

"You dirty, rotten coward. You make me sick," I fumed. "You always did love killing innocent animals, didn't you? You think hunting makes you a man, don't you? Well, not to me, it doesn't."

Twice he tried to interrupt my tirade and both times I cut him dead.

"I would've bet my life on you, Matt. That's how blind and stupid I am. But you did do it, didn't you? You shot Gracie's fawn."

Matt's face turned slowly from white to red. He dropped his gaze, not able to look me in the eye.

"I can explain," he muttered feebly.

"Oh, no you can't, because I'm not listening. I'll never forgive you for this, Matt. Never!"

I had to leave the room then because I was afraid I was going to smack his guilty face. Slamming the woodshed door with all my might, I headed back out to the barn.

Starr whinnied joyously to see me back so soon. I leaned my head against his and he pressed a little closer. What excuse could Matt possibly have for shooting a little wild creature, especially a baby? I hated the despicable thing he'd done.

More than ever now, I was determined to become a vet. Not just a vet, but the best animal doctor in the world.

I hugged Starr's long warm nose and he nuzzled my neck with his velvety lips. His whiskers tickled my chin and made me shiver.

He tried to comfort me with little horsey sounds, even though he couldn't know what was wrong, being a horse after all. Still, more than any human being ever could have, he helped me.

When I went back into the house, the Muggins had gone.

Uncle Herb was the first to speak.

"Everybody makes mistakes, Maggie, even your best friend."

"I have no best friend," I said, and went to bed.

*   *   *

The next day, I stopped in at Dr. Wiley's veterinary clinic at Four Corners to get some medicine for the fawn. His small office was pretty messy. The desk and swivel chair were scratched and old, and horse hair stuffing spilled out of the leather couch. But that didn't matter. The only things I was interested in were the certificates on the walls — his medical degrees. In my mind's eye I could visualize a framed document that read, *Doctor Margaret Rose Emerson, D.V.M.*

That night after supper, Aunt Marg and Gracie and I went down to the barn to check on our patient in the temporary pen that Uncle Herb had built and lined with clean straw.

The little fawn stood on wobbly legs, her enormous eyes staring at us curiously. She didn't seem to be the least bit afraid. I think she knew we wouldn't hurt her for the world.

It was then that Aunt Marg finally made me listen to what had taken place the day Petunia was shot.

"It was a misty morning, Margaret, and Matt was out hunting before dawn. He said the fog was so thick you could cut it with a knife, and the bush was as dark as night. Then he caught a glimpse of what he thought was a coyote and he shot it for fear it might be rabid."

As she spoke she scratched the fawn's white bib and it lifted its head for more. She continued without looking at me.

"Matt says he'll bring fresh cedar boughs in from the bush every day so your uncle won't have to. He wants to do all he can to help. And Jessie says Matt's hung his gun over the mantlepiece. She says he's learned his lesson and he's given up hunting for good and all, Margaret."

"I'll believe that when I see it," I answered coldly, still angry and unforgiving.

21

The conspiracy

"Aunt Marg, I need to talk to you, woman-to-woman."

"About Matt?" she asked, too quickly.

"No." I felt a twinge of pain. "About Uncle Herb."

We were in the barn gathering eggs. Uncle Herb and Gracie had gone to Four Corners for the mail. They'd taken the horse and buggy even though the pickup's tires were all fixed and the car was off the blocks. Uncle Herb was afraid to take either one in case they got stuck in the spring mud.

Aunt Marg drew an anxious breath.

"What is it, Margaret?" she asked.

I decided not to beat around the bush.

"Uncle Herb's going deaf, isn't he? You're a nurse, so you must've noticed."

She sighed and set the egg basket down.

"Yes, Margaret, I have. For a long time now I've tried to fool myself into thinking he was just getting crotchety in his old age — we're not getting any younger, you know — but I've finally had to come to terms with it."

"What do you mean, 'come to terms'? Have you decided to just accept it? Why haven't you talked it over with me?" I couldn't keep the annoyance out of my voice.

"I didn't want to worry you, old sweetheart."

She reached out and squeezed my hand.

"I thought you had enough on your plate, what with algebra and chemistry and physics and all those foreign languages. Fifth form is hard enough for anybody, let alone a sixteen-year-old."

"Have you mentioned it to Uncle Herb?"

"I've tried to broach the subject, but every time I do he gets stubborn and insists he hears fine. He just won't admit anything's wrong. Not for a moment."

"Well, I think Dr. Tom should be consulted."

"I've already hinted in that direction. I said I thought we all needed a good checkup."

"What'd he say?"

"He said to go ahead, but not to make any arrangements for him. He says he's fine and dandy."

"Well, there's only one way then. We'll have to trick him into it."

"That's easier said than done. We'd have a deuce of a time hoodwinking him into that office. He'd see right through us."

"Oh, I don't know about that. We sure pulled the wool over his eyes with that fake chewing tobacco" — we both smiled at the memory — "and I can be pretty sneaky when I want to be. That's something else I inherited from my grandma. Ma says Grandma Marshall could trick a dog out of a bone full of marrow."

Just then Petunia started bleating and thumping around in her pen. That meant she must've heard Starr coming up the lane, which in

116

turn to her meant Gracie would soon be there to feed her.

Sure enough, Uncle Herb was just taking Starr out of the shafts when Aunt Marg and I came out into the barnyard. As soon as Starr saw me, he began prancing around like a colt. His flying tail almost swished the egg basket out of Aunt Marg's grasp.

"For mercy sakes, Starr, act your age!" she scolded, transferring the basket from one arm to the other. "Get him into the barn, Margaret, and calm him down. And make sure he doesn't step on any of my ladies. The dear little souls did a lovely job today. They laid twice as many brown eggs as white. Gracie, you go and feed Petunia before she kicks her pen into kindling wood."

"Got any orders for me, sergeant?" chuckled Uncle Herb.

"Yes. Pull your earflaps down before you catch your death of cold. It's not spring yet, you know. You sounded wheezy last night. I'll have to dose you up with spirits of camphor tonight."

He grinned his natural, happy grin and did as he was told.

Then Aunt Marg said, "Did you remember to get me a writing tablet and a bottle of blue ink and some two cent stamps from the post office, Herb? I've owed that sister of mine a letter for a week."

Uncle Herb's grin faded and he lifted an earflap and asked peevishly, "What's that you say? Speak up, woman. You're all the time muttering."

That did it. There and then I decided to see Dr. Tom about Uncle Herb as soon as I could.

*   *   *

The very next day after school was finished, I marched over to Dr. Tom's office on Main Street.

Unlike Dr. Wiley's office, Dr. Tom's was new and had nice furnishings. His medical certificates lining the walls were all framed in brass. But of course not one of them ended in the magic letters *D.V.M.*

His inner office door opened and he escorted a worried-looking young mother with a crying baby in her arms to the door, earnestly giving her advice along the way. On his way back he saw me sitting there.

"Margaret. Well, and how's your old straw hat?"

I followed him into his office and sat on the big leather chair opposite him.

"I'm fine, Dr. Tom. It's Uncle Herb I've come to see you about."

"What's that rascal been up to now?" he said, leaning back in his swivel chair and clasping his hands behind his head.

So I told him all the signs Aunt Marg and I had noticed: not hearing the crystal set when it was as clear as a cowbell; refusing to speak on the phone, even to me; pretending to understand questions by guessing at the answers; unconsciously cupping his ear to catch what was being said; acting cranky and crotchety, which wasn't like him at all.

"I think he's going deaf," I finished despairingly.

The doctor's expression was sober now. He frowned and shook his head.

"He's certainly got all the classic symptoms," he said. "Well, I'll have to get him in here and have a look at him. Then if your suspicions are confirmed,

I'll make an appointment with a colleague of mine who's an ear specialist at the Toronto General. There are some fine hearing devices on the market today, Margaret, so don't look so distressed."

"The trouble is, Uncle Herb won't admit he's got a problem. And he refuses to come to see you. The only way we'd ever get him here would be to trick him into it. Aunt Marg and I are stumped. We thought you might have some ideas . . . "

"Hm."

He combed thin strands of grey hair thoughtfully across the top of his shiny head with his fingers.

"Let's put our thinking caps on," he said at last.

We came up with several notions and rejected them one by one. Suddenly I had a flash of inspiration.

"I think I've got it," I cried. "I'll have a terrible attack of appendicitis when Aunt Marg is off somewhere with Gracie and can't be reached."

"You're a genius, girl, or a corker, as Herb would say. That ought to work. He'll do anything for you."

* * *

The following Saturday, Aunt Marg went over to check on Mabel Raggett, taking Gracie with her to play with Luella.

Mabel was expecting a baby soon and wouldn't let anybody but Aunt Marg touch her. She said she didn't trust doctors as far as she could throw them.

Well, as luck would have it, the baby came early and Aunt Marg had to stay on.

After supper, while Uncle Herb was out doing the milking, I phoned Dr. Tom.

"Is tonight all right?" I asked, explaining that Aunt Marg was out of reach.

"I'll be right here in my office, Margaret. I won't set foot out the door," he promised.

When Uncle Herb came in, he found me doubled up over the dishpan, the dishes only half done, moaning and holding my side. He set the bucket down so hard a wave of milk slopped over the side.

"Maggie! Maggie! What ails you, girl?"

"I think it's my appendix. Oh, please, Uncle Herb, call Dr. Tom."

He didn't hesitate for a split second. Quickly, he went to the phone, gave it a crank, and barked at Central, "Got an emergency here, Nora. Put me through to Dr. Tom pronto."

Dr. Tom, of course, said to bring me right in.

After examining me and giving me some sugar pills, the doctor explained to Uncle Herb that the pills would take the inflammation down, and he assured him I was in no immediate danger.

He spoke in a normal tone of voice, but he had his back to us while he made up the prescription. Then he turned towards us.

"Would you repeat those instructions, Herb," he asked innocently. "I want them followed to the letter."

"What letter?" Uncle Herb looked puzzled.

"Didn't you hear what I said, Herb?"

He spoke louder this time.

"You was mumbling with your backside facing me. I'm not a mind reader," snapped Uncle Herb.

"I wasn't mumbling, Herb. I was speaking very clearly. Did you hear me, Margaret?"

I nodded, still clutching my side.

"Considering Margaret heard me and you

didn't, and since you're here anyway, I might as well kill two birds with one stone."

In a jiffy, before Uncle Herb had a chance to object, Dr. Tom was peering into his ear with a long thin flashlight.

I continued to hold my side and look pitiful because I was determined Uncle Herb would never find out the whole thing was a conspiracy.

When he was finished his examination, Dr. Tom said, "I want you to see a friend of mine at Toronto General, Herb. He's an ear specialist and I'm sure he can help you."

"I'm not going to no hospital."

Uncle Herb got up and shrugged on his coat.

"Are you feeling all right now, Maggie? We got to get back to Green Meadows. I've got work to do."

"I think I can make it," I said weakly, keeping up the act.

Dr. Tom helped me on with my coat and ordered me solemnly to take two pills every four hours and to come back to see him on Monday.

"I'm going to Toronto next Thursday morning, Herb. I've got two patients to check up on, so I'll pick you up at eight sharp."

Before Uncle Herb could open his mouth to object, the doctor reached for his phone and waved us out the door.

*   *   *

Uncle Herb went with Dr. Tom and was given a hearing aid. But the minute he got home, he put it at the back of the sideboard drawer, and there it stayed.

No one could persuade him to give it a try. He swore it was the most foolish gadget he'd ever wasted money on, a piece of tomfoolery, if ever there was one.

Well, at least he never found out how it was that he came to acquire that piece of tomfoolery in the first place.

22

Atonement

As the end of the school year drew closer, my studies crowded everything else out of my mind. I was determined to excel because I knew I had to have high marks to qualify for the Ontario Veterinary College in Guelph, especially since I was a girl.

I was prepared to do all the work alone, but in the end Mr. Bannister really surprised me with all kinds of help and encouragement. I couldn't get over it.

Dora just wagged her finger in my face and said, "I told you there was a lot of good in Dusty."

I didn't go home to the farm every weekend because I found I could concentrate better in the Hares' house.

Gracie didn't mean to bother me, but she was such a natural chatterbox that she nearly drove me to distraction. If she wasn't talking to one of us, she was rattling on to Silky. Then I'd get mad and yell at her and that would upset Aunt Marg, so I decided to spend more time in Shelburne until after the exams.

Of course I still had to endure Rabbit's riddles.

"Here's one for the highly eddicated. Who invented fractions, Maggie?" he chortled, sure that he had me this time.

"Henry the Eighth!" I dropped my head into the middle of my chemistry book with a thud and a long-suffering sigh.

Undaunted, he tried again.

"What two words have the most letters, Meg?"

"The post office!" I groaned, and threw up my hands, cracking my elbow on the table's edge.

"Ow!" I yelled, and began rubbing the pain out of my arm.

"What's the trouble, Meggie?" asked Rabbit innocently.

"I hit my funny bone," I snapped.

"Then why ain't you laughing?" he snickered.

"Rabbit Roger Hare!" Dora came at him with the broomstick. "Why don't you save your breath to cool your porridge?"

Rabbit slunk away looking offended.

*   *   *

After several weekends of not going to the farm, I began to feel pretty lonely. So one incredibly beautiful May day I got a ride home to Green Meadows with Zach and Eva.

As we bumped up our rutted lane, I saw Starr across the meadow grazing on some fresh spring greenery. I leapt out before we'd even stopped properly and ran to the split-rail fence. Cupping my hands around my lips, I blew our secret signal — the silent whistle that only he could hear.

Starr's head jerked up like a jack-in-the-box and then he charged across the field towards me, his tail and mane flying like sails in the wind. Fifteen hundred pounds of horseflesh stopped just inches from my toes, sending clods of earth flying in the air.

I hugged Starr's head and kissed his cheek and rubbed the star on his nose. He whinnied and snorted and vibrated his lips, making that peculiar flurried sound that only horses do.

"Take him to the barn and water him, Maggie!" called Uncle Herb from the porch.

As soon as I walked into the barn I noticed Petunia's pen was empty. Quickly I put fresh water out for Starr and gave him a feed of oats before I rushed inside.

Aunt Marg was scurrying around the kitchen looking like the cat that had swallowed the canary. Gracie was jumping up and down, her red braids bobbing with excitement.

"Matt's helping me to teach Petunia how to be wild again," she cried, her eyes all aglow.

"Where is he?" I asked skeptically.

"He's perched up in a tree for the night with his gun, watching every move Petty makes. He wouldn't let me stay because he said I might go to sleep and fall off the branch, but I wouldn't. I know I wouldn't."

I didn't question her any further. Instead, after both Gracie and Uncle Herb had gone to bed, I talked to Aunt Marg.

"Do you think it's possible for a tame animal to go back into the wild?" I asked apprehensively.

"Well, I'm no judge of that, Margaret, but Matt did talk it over with Dr. Wiley, and Dr. Wiley did say it'd been successfully done before."

She stirred and creamed our nightly cocoa, then sat down beside me at the table.

"Matt's determined to redeem himself in your eyes, Margaret."

She squeezed my hand and I couldn't help but

notice how small and chubby hers was compared to my long, lean fingers.

"The least you can do is give him that chance," she added.

I decided to wait and see, so I dropped the subject.

I was content just to be home again.

Green Meadows. What a terrific name Aunt Marg and Uncle Herb had chosen for their farm years ago. It fairly sang of spring!

23
News from home

When I got back to the Hares' house, there was a letter propped up on the sugar bowl with my name on it. Also, there was a note pinned to the curtain explaining that Dora and Rabbit had gone to see Horace and Mabel, Rabbit's brother and his wife.

The handwriting on the envelope was Josie's, so I tore it open eagerly.

149 Rose Avenue
Toronto 1, Ontario
May 9, 1932

Dear Peg,
You're the one who owes yours truly a letter, but I know you haven't got time to write because you're studying for your finals. I am, too, but I'm only in middle school, so it's not so important that I get high marks. I don't know what I want to be anyway, so I don't care as long as I pass. I'm glad I didn't skip a year like you.

Anyway, that's not what I'm writing about. I've got some news that I thought you'd find interesting, if not astonishing! Remember Rodney Gallaugher who was Andrew's best man at the wedding? You know, the handsome one who had a crush on you? Well, guess what? Rodney's saved up enough money by working at the Sunlight Soap Works to pay his way through college. He's going to Guelph, just like you! He wants to be a zoologist or a biologist. Something like that. Anyway, the thing that matters is, you'll both be in the same college. Talk about coincidence! When Olive told him you were going to be there too, she said you should've seen his face light up.

By the way, since we're on the subject of boys, I am *not* going around with Gilbert any more. Remember I told you how much he reminded me of Matt Muggins? Well he does, but he isn't . . . like Matt I mean. He turned out to be really nasty. A couple of times I caught him giving Bobby and Davey a smack when no one was looking. I feel like smacking them myself sometimes when they act like little fiends, but I told him not to lay a hand on them because they're not his brothers. He said that if we ever got married, they would be and then he'd fix them good. So I told him I never wanted to see him again. He went slamming out the front door, making the glass rattle. Thank goodness Pa wasn't home. That's his pride and joy, that stained glass window in the front door. I thought I'd miss Gilbert, but I don't miss him the least little bit. I'm really glad to be rid of him. He even pulled my hair once!

Actually, I miss Matt Muggins more, and that's funny because he never was my boyfriend and I don't know him all that well. But there's something special about him. Does he ever ask about me? Maybe I'll see him when I come up in the summer. Don't forget you invited me. I'm dying to meet the Hares and eat off their newspaper tablecloth. Anyway, Peg, say hello to them for me and give my love to everybody on the farm, including Starr! Also, would you please mention my name to Matt once in a while and tell him sort of casually that I'm coming up this summer?

Please write when you have a minute and tell me all the news. Is Uncle Herb enjoying his hearing aid? Does it work with the crystal set? I'll bet he's his old happy self again.

I have to go now because the little kids are fighting over the biscuits. Ma says I'm in charge when she's out now that Harry and Jenny have work after school in Black's Funeral Parlours. They don't have to go near the dead people. They just do the sweeping and dusting in the sitting room. Ma said it's a heathenish job for young folks, but Pa says it'll teach them what life is all about. And besides, the pay's good— fifty cents a day each. You should hear some of the stories they tell about eerie moans and groans coming from the coffins when the lids are shut and there's no one else around. I'm sure they'll give you an earful when you come home for your summer visit.

I really have to go now.

Your loving sister,
Josephine-Frances

P.S. Do you like my name hyphenated? I do, so don't call me Josie any more. J-F

P.P.S. I forgot to ask about Petunia. Gracie told us all about her pet deer in a cute letter she wrote the whole family. It must be incredible to have a pet deer. But what will they do with it when it gets big? Pa says they'll have to eat it and he hopes Uncle Herb remembers to put some in the icehouse for him because he's very partial to venison. But I said that sounds pretty cannibalistic and you won't allow it. You'd have the right to forbid it, because you saved its life. And I'd agree with you!

XXXOOO J-F-E

I read the letter several times and blushed every time I came to the part about Rodney. One other thing about my reaction to Josie's—Josephine-Frances' —letter: I didn't feel a speck of jealousy where Matt was concerned. I used to be as mean as a dog with a bone about Matt. Now I seemed to have finally dropped the bone. Perhaps hearing about Rodney had something to do with it.

*   *   *

By the time I got around to writing back, I was able to include some good news about Petunia. After many weeks of patient work on Matt's part, the young buck (as it had turned out to be after all!) had finally run off with a doe into the bush and was never seen again. This made Gracie feel sad, but she knew it was for the best.

I felt badly to have to report that Uncle Herb wasn't using his hearing aid at all.

24

On my way

The finals were hard, but this time I was ready for them. Still, by the time I'd finished the last exam I was so tired I could hardly keep my eyes open.

Dora gave me a pitying smile as I dragged myself in the door at the end of the week.

"I've got a nice supper on, Meggie," she said encouragingly. "Pork bones plum full of juicy meat, boiled new potatoes about the size of agates and fresh water cress. I gathered the cress myself by the creek just this morning. I was down there hunting for pearls in the freshwater shell fish. Myrtle Stromberg found a lovely pink one yesterday."

"It sounds good," I said, stifling a yawn. "Is there time for me to have a bath before supper, Dora? The cold water might pep me up."

"There's plenty of hot water. I've had the Kitchen Queen on all afternoon cooking up a storm."

Dora helped me carry pail after pail of near-boiling water from the stove's reservoir into the little chamber beside the pantry.

It was a tiny, narrow room Rabbit had made by lopping off a piece of the kitchen. The big, copper tub and the old-fashioned toilet with the pullchain water closet above it took up so much space that you could hardly turn around.

I added cold water from the faucet until the temperature was just right. Then I slid down into the warm soft water and let the weariness soak out of my bones.

That was one thing I was really going to miss on the farm. There we still took our baths in the kitchen in a corrugated washtub that I could barely fit into any more. I had to sit with my knees drawn up right under my chin. It wasn't very relaxing.

* * *

The following afternoon I began packing my things into the back seat of the Model A.

Dora stood watching me, looking downright depressed, so I said, "I'll probably be back so often I'll wear my welcome out."

"Fat chance!" she snorted.

Then she cranked and I choked, and off I went in a cloud of dust.

Aunt Marg was making a batch of raisin tea biscuits when I arrived at the farm.

"Well, Margaret," she tried not to sound anxious as she poked some extra raisins in the soft dough with her fingertip, "aren't you going to tell me how you did?"

I felt better than I did the night before, so I answered cheerfully, "Oh, all right I guess, Aunt Marg. But every single exam was extra hard."

Uncle Herb came in just as I was speaking.

"What's that you say, Maggie?"

He patted his round stomach and sniffed the first batch of biscuits baking in the stove's hot oven. I kissed him hello on his red-whiskered cheek

— and had to lean right over to do so. I was about four inches taller than him now.

"I was just telling Aunt Marg," I shouted in his direction, "that I found the exams really difficult this time."

"Well, just put them out of your mind now, Maggie, they're over and done with. You look pale and piqued. Come away down to the barn with me and have a look at the old girl's horn. She hurt it somehow when she was out in the pasture and it's bleeding so bad I might have to ask Doc Wiley to saw it off."

Good old Uncle Herb. He knew the pungent smell of the barn would put colour into my cheeks and make me forget everything else.

I went straight to work on Flora's injured horn. It didn't look so bad once I'd cleaned it and doused it with iodine. I wrapped it in strips of flannel and hoped she wouldn't rub the bandage off before the horn had a chance to heal.

Next, Uncle Herb and I walked out into the flowery meadowland to find Fern and Fancy. They mooed softly when we approached and gazed at us with their placid, trusting brown eyes. I patted each of them on their wide wet noses. Fern, who was still a baby, licked my hand and tried to suck my finger.

"Animals are lovely, aren't they, Uncle Herb," I said as the two cows went back to their munching.

"Lovely," he agreed, and he took hold of my hand the way he used to when I was a child.

We walked quietly hand in hand over to the grove of trees where Starr was sure to be. And there he was, upside down, playing, his great hairy hooves thrashing the air as he rolled about ecstatically in a patch of purple clover.

He was having so much fun, we got within forty feet of him before he noticed us. His long white lashes fluttered when he spied me.

Whomp! went his huge body over to one side. He gathered himself up on his strong legs, first the front and then the back, and began galloping around us in crazy circles, whinnying his head off. Finally he came to me and buried his snout in my arms.

"It's a wonder he ain't good for nothing, the way you spoil him," laughed Uncle Herb as he gave Starr's sinewy neck a long stroke.

"It works just the opposite, Uncle Herb," I shouted over the horse's loud snorts. "Animals need love just like people. It makes them better, not worse."

"Well, I'll take your word for it, Maggie. Starr sure bears you out on that. He's the best horse in the county. And you'll be the best vet in the county, that's for certain. You got more feel for creatures than anybody I know."

"I hope you're right, Uncle Herb."

We started back to the house. Just then, Gracie saw us and came racing towards us, whirling her school bag over her head.

"My gosh you're getting tall," I said, giving her a sisterly hug. "And you've run off all your baby fat."

I couldn't get over how much she'd grown in a few short weeks. She giggled at my lopsided compliment, then we each grabbed one of Uncle Herb's rough hands and, swinging our arms in unison, we all three skipped like crazy kids across the meadow.

*   *   *

On a balmy night early in June, the phone rang while we were all sitting around the table dawdling over our tea. I jumped up to answer it, thinking it'd be Eva.

"Margaret," Nora said, her voice sounding more important than usual, "I have a long-distance call for you from Shelburne. Hold on and I'll put it through."

After a couple of clicks, a voice inquired, "Miss Emerson?"

I recognized Mr. Bannister's voice at once and responded with a breathless, "Yes?"

"I have some news for you. Are you sitting down?"

"No, sir," I answered stupidly, and promptly sat with a thump on the chair under the phone.

"Well, now. This is unofficial. Entirely unofficial, you understand."

My heart gave a lurch.

"Yes, Mr. Bannister?"

I turned towards the table so the others could hear.

Then I listened to what Mr. Bannister had to say.

I seemed to have lost my own voice and was able to respond only with strange little grunts.

Finally I managed to say thank you, and we both hung up.

"What is it, Margaret?" cried Aunt Marg anxiously as soon as the phone was back on the hook.

"The suspense is killin' me," declared Uncle Herb.

"Peggy, Peggy, tell us what the principal said," begged Gracie.

I felt my face stretch into a huge, triumphant

grin. Usually I played down how smart I was so I wouldn't sound conceited, but this time I couldn't help bragging.

"Mr. Bannister says I'm top of the class. Maybe even top of the whole county."

Saying it made the news sink in and my eyes suddenly filled with tears. My wet lashes swept up and down my spectacles, making them all smeary.

"Oh, Margaret, my old sweetheart!" Aunt Marg jumped up and hugged me and took off my glasses to wipe them on her apron.

Uncle Herb dabbed his eyes with his checkered handkerchief, blew his nose with a loud honk, and said, "Maggie, girl, I'm so happy for you that if I had a tail I'd wag it."

That made Gracie screech with laughter. Then she grabbed my hands and danced me around in a circle as though she was playing *Ring Around the Rosy*.

"And that's not all," I cried breathlessly as we collapsed back into our chairs. "Mr. Bannister wants me to be valedictorian at the graduation ceremonies."

"Oh, Margaret! What an honour!" Aunt Marg's round cheeks flushed with pride.

"What's a valedic . . . valedictory?" asked Gracie.

"Valedictorian, Gracie. It's the person who gives the speech on graduation day."

"Oh, boy, I'll be able to help you, Peg," cried my nine-year-old sister. "I made a speech last week all about when I was young and lived in the city. The teacher gave me an E for excellent. I'm really good at composition."

She was, too. And she helped me a lot.

* * *

The great day arrived and Josie and my parents came all the way from Toronto to attend the ceremony.

In my address I thanked them all — my two families, my faithful friends, and Dusty Bannister. I called him that right out loud by mistake and my schoolmates hooted and laughed and stamped their feet.

I nearly died of embarrassment at my slip, until I saw Mr. Bannister laughing too.

When it was all over and we graduates held our fifth form diplomas in our trembling hands, our families descended upon us.

My pa, looking tall and handsome in his new straw boater, his dark eyes glittering behind thick horn-rimmed spectacles, was the first to congratulate me.

"You're a credit to us all, Peg," he said in a choked-up voice, then he kissed me self-consciously on the forehead.

Ma and Aunt Marg, looking for all the world like twins with their red hair and green silk crepe de chine dresses, hugged and kissed me tearfully.

And Josie — beautiful Josie — slipped her arm around my waist and whispered, "I'm ever so proud of you, Peg."

That meant a lot to me, coming from Josie, whom I had always envied for her extraordinary beauty.

Next it was Uncle Herb's turn. He looked unusually splendid in his blue serge suit with his father's gold watch chain looped across his stomach.

He held out his arms to me as he used to do

when I was a little girl and I went into them and leaned down to receive his kiss.

"That was a mighty fine speech, Maggie," he said in a hoarse voice.

"Did you hear it, Uncle Herb?" I asked incredulously.

"Every blinkin' word," he said, pointing to his ear.

There, almost hidden by his fuzzy red side-whiskers, was the hearing aid.

"Oh, Uncle Herb, thanks for wearing it," I said.

"Best danged gadget I ever had," he answered, proud as punch of himself.

Now the Muggins family surrounded me.

Jessie and Zach offered warm congratulations. Eva squealed and hugged me. Matt looked awkward.

We still hadn't spoken since the shooting incident. Self-consciously, he wiped his light brown hair out of his pale blue eyes.

"Good going, Marg," he said.

"Thanks, Matt."

We shook hands and wordlessly mended our fences.

Then Josie came over and she and Matt smiled shyly at each other — and I didn't mind a bit.

While all this was going on, Rabbit and Dora had stayed in the background.

I saw them over Ma's head and I beckoned for them to join us.

Dora gave me an unaccustomed kiss.

"You did fine, Meg," she said. "We're mighty proud of you."

Rabbit squeezed my hand.

"Meggie," he said in a loud but conspiratorial

voice, "now that you've proved how smart you are, I got a question."

Everybody within earshot stopped talking to listen, which is exactly what he intended them to do.

"Yes, Rabbit?"

He'd caught me off guard, so I fell neatly into his trap. I should've known better by the way his ears and nose were twitching.

"Well, now, I'd be pleased to know" — he enjoyed being the centre of attention, so he dragged it out — "what come first, the chicken or the egg?"

For the first time ever, I was stumped.

Rabbit slapped his knee and shouted gleefully, *"Gotcha!"*

When the laughter finally died down, I knew I had to come up with some kind of an answer.

"I don't know what came first, the chicken or the egg, Rabbit. That's what I'm going to university for — to find out. And when I do, you'll be the first to know."

Epilogue

I finally received my Doctorate in Veterinary Medicine in 1936 when I was twenty-one years old.

I began my practice as Dr. Wiley's assistant. When he decided to retire in 1937, I took over the practice and hung up my shingle — literally.

Matthew made it for me.

On a fine sheet of pine he carefully carved my full name, and then added those three magic letters, *D.V.M.*

One year later, that same Matthew Muggins and my own dear sister Josephine were married in Toronto.

She was the most beautiful bride I'd ever seen, and he was the proudest groom.

*   *   *

And Starr, my wonderful four-footed friend, lived to the ripe old age of thirty-eight, a record for a Clydesdale, or any other horse for that matter.

But that didn't make it any easier to say goodbye.

BERNICE THURMAN HUNTER

Bernice Thurman Hunter won the 1990 Vicky Metcalf Award for her contribution to Canadian children's literature. She is best known for her Booky trilogy — stories about growing up during the Great Depression. The first in the series, *That Scatterbrain Booky*, won the 1981 IODE Award, and has been made into a play.

As well as the Margaret series, Bernice has written *Lamplighter*, which paints an authentic picture of life in Northern Ontario during the 1880s, and *The Railroader*, the exciting adventures of a boy in the late 1940s who dreams of becoming a railroad engineer. Her books have been translated into many languages and are read around the world.

Bernice enjoys meeting her readers as she visits schools and libraries across Canada.